The Citadel

The Citadel

John Reinhard Dizon

Published 2021 by Next Chapter
Cover art by Cover Mint
Back cover texture by David M. Schrader, used under license from Shutterstock.com

Chapter One

The Hole in the Wall restaurant in Dublin was a centuries-old pub that had been lavishly refurbished along its journey into the 21st century. A sign above the entrance announcing the Mc Caffreys Lounge and Bar gave credit where due, and the family-owned business was all about Irish hospitality toward tourists and locals who streamed through its halls. It was early evening along Blackhorse Avenue, and two groups stood on opposite ends of the sidewalk for a short while before signaling they would meet inside. They had reserved tables and were sure their business discussion would be drowned by the lively crowd.

The lovely waitress with the tight-fitting 'Keep Calm' souvenir T-shirt was wary of the situation as she arrived to take orders at the three tables in the rear corner. The six black-leathered men were grim-faced, one man at each table on either side of the corner where the other four were seated. This smelled of a gang meeting but she knew far better than to call attention to the scene. She knew of men who had their faces bashed in for such indiscretion.

"Jack feckin' Gawain," the leader of the four-man team grinned, his lieutenant staring across the table at their guests. "How the mighty have fallen. Ye know, Mickey Donahue has it in the back of his mind this whole thing is a set-up, and I can't say I blame him. I'll tell ye, Mc Namara, if anything at all goes sideways on this deal, yer the first one to go, right before yer entire family."

"Hey, blow it out yer ass," Daniel Mc Namara grumbled. He was a tall, stocky man with a large skull that earned him the name Bobblehead. "I got people standin' behind me as well. They cleared him before they put him together with me, you should know that. Man's got a right to earn, everyone knows that. Maybe the Raghead's got a problem with him but we don't. He sets up shop in East Belfast on commission, it's extra income for all of us. You already know that."

"You got questions, you ask me, I'm right here," Gawain glared at them. He was a powerfully-built man with close-cropped dark hair and ruggedly handsome features, his dark eyes as agates. "I've got as much to worry about as anyone here, even more. If I go back inside I'll never see the light of day again. I got the Brits and the peelers so far up me arse, I fart Union Jacks. They gave me parole for takin' somebody out for 'em on condition I went clean or left the UK. I'm still here, and my buffers are so thick they can't touch me with a pole. I got no choice but for it to stay that way."

"Yeah, we heard," Malice scowled. He was one of the two captains of the Donahue Gang, the biggest meth dealers in Dublin. "We also heard that Jackie Raghead thinks you did in one of his guys to get yer pass. Nobody gives a piss about a Prod[1] gettin' smoked, but doin' hits for the peelers, now that's a big two-way street."

"Ye know I'm not tellin' ye who I did in, that'd sign me own death warrant. If they could prove Raghead to be right, I'd be in the harbor right now. He made the beef just to move me outta the picture, and everyone knows it."

"Besides, he did the work for the Brits, not the peelers," Danny insisted. "Look, I thought this was all sorted out. You want us to walk out and start over some other time?"

"Nay, this shite is happenin' tonight. It's all set up. I answer to the Big Mick on this. I just wanna make sure everyone knows where we all stand. If anything goes wrong, Danny, there's people goin' into the ground behind ye. Ye'd best keep it in mind."

---

1. Protestant

"Tonight!" Danny protested. "I've gotta go back and clear it with my people! I'm just on authority to seal the deal, not move ahead on it."

"There's nothing to clear," Malice insisted. "We're movin' this across the border from Dundalk up to Armagh. It's gotta happen tonight, our connections with the Gardai guarantee they can keep the road clear until midnight. You need to make sure we get through those biker bastards past the border on the 177. Once we hit Armagh, we switch trucks and bring the merchandise into Belfast. It's a thousand for each of ye, plus it'll assure us yer both sound."

"I've got nothin' on tap fer tonight," Gawain sat back in his seat as the waitress brought a round of beers to the next table. "Your call, Danny Boy."

"*The pipes, the pipes are calling*," the lieutenant, Venom, crooned mockingly.

"Feckin' comedians," Danny snarled. "Okay, I gotta make me call."

"No way," Malice retorted. "We got fifty thousand ridin' on this shipment. Call gets intercepted, all of us are goin' up the river, and it's the Mick who takes the bath. No phone contact until we hit the border. Both sides probably have agreements not to intercept each other's transmissions out that way."

"What th' feck," Danny grew upset. "Ye don't think I had anything else besides this goin' tonight? We were just supposed t'get sorted out and get set for a run."

"Schedule change. Run happens tonight, are ye in or out?"

"An' what happens when we get to Belfast?" Danny asked as they passed out the mugs.

"Ye call yer friends an' tell 'em we're in town."

The men finished their beers and headed to the parking lot, the four Irishmen leading the way for Jack and Danny as the two escorts followed them out. Malice pulled out his remote control, activating the car alarm on his late-model minivan. The emergency lights flashed as the eight men climbed into the vehicle and pulled out of the parking lot. Within minutes they cruised onto the highway and were en route along the R132 North towards the M1 to the Northern Ireland border.

"So you were contracted by the Brits to take out some enemy of the State," Malice asked, passing a joint to Gawain as they sat face-to-face on the seats lining both walls of the comfortable van. "You sure they don't have ye on call in case a need arises in future?"

"Are ye questionin' Danny Boy's intelligence, him bringin' me out to meet up with you fellows for a chat like this?" Gawain took a deep drag of the joint as Venom opened up a small baggie of crystal meth.

"Not at all, fella, it just seems a waste that they'd put ye in trainin' for that sort of work an' then just let ye walk free and clear once all was said and done," Malice replied.

"Aye, and they know I had a proclivity for such work, or they wouldn't have asked me in the first place. It wasn't like they'd culled H-Block for a babe in the woods."

"Your reputation precedes ye, Magic Jack," Venom snorted a line of meth before passing the switchblade and the baggie to him. "Maybe ye'd see fit to make a couple of fellows disappear for us now and again, for the right price."

"Take care, brother," Danny scowled. "Jack's with us now, it's not right for ye to be recruitin' from our crew, and everyone knows it."

"Settle down, Danny Boy," Malice replied. "We know how things are. Ye know we send fellows out in pairs to handle those kind of chores. If you and Jack make a good show of yourselves tonight, there'd be no reason why we wouldn't invite you both back."

"You all know I'm with Billy Shamrock, I can't wander off and take contracts without his say. I do appreciate the offer, though, and I will keep it in mind if I'm ever forced to go South for whatever reason in future."

"An' you're with Shamrock too, I take it," Malice looked at Gawain as his eyes bulged from the lightning shot of meth that hit his brain pan.

"Shite," Gawain blinked, his eyes watering. "That's some good stuff. Aye, well, I'm with Danny, and he's under Mick, so that's the beginning and end of it."

"So let me get this straight," Danny passed the joint to one of the gunmen. "You brought us along to make sure you can get from Dundalk to Armagh. Why the hell didn't you let Billy Sham know what was on before we got here? We could've had an escort awaiting."

"It all happened too quick," Venom explained. "We'd come here to talk just like we said. Only our cook got a big batch completed and the Mick didn't want it sittin' idle in one spot. He made a decision t'move it and the job got dumped in our laps. Look, we know Billy Sham's got the cash t'make th' buy, an' I'm sure he can move it just as quick as he can take possession. Ye've got enough tweakers in East Belfast to unload it on in less than a day, at worst. We don't foresee any problems, but if some cowboys out of Armagh decide to try a carjack, it'll avoid a lot of bloodshed if you can defuse a situation."

"So you think if a carjack team comes against us, I'll just have 'em wait a mo' while I get Billy Sham on the line, eh?"

"Aye, something like that," Malice managed a chuckle.

They crossed the Dundalk Western Bypass onto the Newry-Dundalk Link Road, then took the B113 into Jonesborough where they began heading south away from the highway. Both Jack and Danny grew apprehensive but said nothing. The streetlamps gave way to dimly-lit country roads, and soon they found themselves bouncing along poorly-paved dirt paths towards a desolate farm area.

"I hope you fellas aren't actin' the maggot," Danny's eyes darted from window to window. "There doesn't seem to be a damn thing out this way."

"We've got a place out here, we're about five minutes out," Venom replied.

Eventually they cruised up to a gateway set within a wire fenceline, and one of the gunmen got out to unlock the entrance. The van rolled in as he relocked the gate and hopped back in, slamming the van shut as they continued towards a shadowy farmhouse ahead. Once again they veered off the dirt road towards a gravel clearing upon which sat a grain silo. The driver pulled alongside it, and both Jack and Danny breathed sighs of relief as the team humped out and headed for the silo. There were far too many stories of gangsters having been taken for one-way rides for reasons unknown to anyone but the gang boss ordering the hit.

"Aw reet, it's all here," one of the gunmen announced as he opened the silo door. He pulled out six suitcases from the silo, passing them along to his cohorts as they loaded them into the minivan.

"Are ye blootered, man?" Danny protested. "What've ye got there, a half million worth of product? If the peelers take us down with this, they'll put us away for the rest of our lives!"

"You don't know what's in the cases, so don't feckin' bother t'ask," Venom replied. "All you two are doin' is catchin' a ride with us. Everyone saw ye leave th' pub with us, ye've got yer alibi."

"Now, I can't tell ye how feckin' relieved that makes me feel," Danny was sarcastic.

It took them a few minutes to load the suitcases into the vehicle, and they were soon on their way back along the dirt road back to the highway. The team was somewhat more cautious, peering out the windows to make sure there were no other cars in the area. They cruised back onto the Newry Bypass as it coursed into the M1 heading north to Dundalk.

"So are ye goin' into Dundalk?" Gawain wondered.

"Nay, we'll stay on the M1 and switch off to A1, then take the A28 to Armagh. When the M1 changes to the N1, we'll have Danny call his people and get us some backup. I don't want t'take the chance of the Brits or the Gardai pickin' up a call from a Southern number along th' border, it might raise a red flag. Can't be too careful."

They saw the signs indicating the northeast turnoff towards Dundalk, and continued on to Newry along the A1. Only when they approached the exit road leading into town, they saw some bikes parked along the access road that began gunning their engines.

"Aw reet, keep yer eyes peeled," Malice warned the driver. "If the drunken bastards're out showin' off, they're liable t'cut in front o' ye."

"Aye, I'm watchin'," the driver grunted.

Their worst fears were realized as the bikers began cruising onto the highway, causing the minivan to slow down to allow them passage. The driver cursed and swore as they continued along at 45 MPH, blocking both lanes so that the vehicle had no way to pass them by. At once they began hitting their parking brakes, and the drug runners knew there was trouble ahead.

"What kind o' hardware ye carryin' here?" Gawain demanded.

"We got Sterlings with silencers," Venom hesitated. "Look, fella, if the Brits are in the air, we're gonna get fecked."

"Ye shoulda thought about that before ye picked me up," Gawain reached under Venom's seat and pulled out the submachine gun. "I go back inside, I'm in fer life. I'm not riskin' me freedom on yer bullshite alibi."

"Feck it all, Jack," Danny's eyes widened. "What're ye gonna do!"

Gawain reached over and threw the door open, then hopped outside with the weapon concealed behind his leg.

"Aw reet, eyeryone outta the van," the leader of the biker team called over, jacking a shotgun as he brandished it in plain view. It was as a signal causing the other three bikers to produce their weapons and jack shells into their chambers. "Keep yer hands where we can see 'em or we take out your windshield. No one has t'get hurt."

Gawain responded by whipping out the Sterling and opening fire on the bikers. The silencer reduced the explosions as a series of pops as the bikers fell screaming from their motorcycles to the ground. He walked over and sprayed each man in the face, causing their brains to splatter across the pavement before he returned to the van.

"What th' feck did ye just do!" Malice was aghast. "Th' feckin' road's still blocked, an' th' first motorcar that comes along'll call the peelers fer sure!"

Gawain replied by opening fire into the minivan. The gangsters screamed as the automatic rounds ripped into their bodies, though the fusillade lasted for less than half a minute. As a precaution, Gawain peered into the van before firing shots into the backs of the front seats.

"Have ye gone feckin' mad, Gawain!" Danny screamed, wiping the gore from his face that had spewed from the torn heads of the men on either side of him.

"You two," Gawain pointed the Sterling at Malice and Venom, sitting next to the dead man draped across their laps. "Ye can buy yerself time by clearin' that road."

"Ye crazy son of a bitch," Malice gasped. "We'll never make it t'Armagh. Ye just fecked us all, ye sick bastard."

Gawain stepped aside, keeping the Sterling trained on the gangsters as they stood the bikes up and rolled them off the road. He then motioned them into the front seats after they pulled the dead men out of the van. Malice gunned the engine and the minivan continued along the way to Armagh.

"What's yer move now, ye sick fecker?" Venom asked hoarsely. "The peelers'll have an APB out as soon as they come across that shite. They'll take the cases, and when the Big Mick finds out what happened…"

"Shut th' feck up an' keep drivin'."

The minivan barely traveled ten miles before helicopters were swirling around the skies above the highway. They saw a convoy of emergency vehicles coming in from South Armagh, and one of the helicopters proceeded to shine a spotlight down on their vehicle.

"All right, pull over," Gawain ordered.

Malice did as he was told, parking the van off to the left side of the road and cutting off the engine. With that, Gawain pulled his Glock-17 from his ankle holster and fired shots into the backs of the heads of both men in the front seats. Danny stared in horror as Gawain unbuckled his holster, rubbed it down to erase his prints, then tossed it into the front seat.

"Now then," Gawain pointed the Glock at Danny's face as they heard the police vans screeching to a halt and barking orders over their loudspeakers. "Here's the deal. There are no witnesses to what happened back there, and no witnesses left in here. These bastards were the only survivors besides us back there, and you managed to pull your hideout before they finished us off here."

"What hideout?" Danny croaked. Gawain rubbed the Glock off and tossed it to Danny just as the van doors were thrown open by the riflemen surrounding the vehicle.

A few hours later, on the other side of the European continent, the man known as William Bruce arrived at a chateau outside of Propriano on the island of Corsica. He was met at a private airstrip by a limousine and driven to the meeting place by a team of three black-suited men. They spoke little English, though appeared jovial and exchanged small talk among themselves. The man seated alongside him offered him a cigarette and a drink from the courtesy bar, both of which he politely declined.

It was generally acknowledged that Gilles 'The Hammer' Marotte had risen to the top of the Corsican Mob by default. At a time when American and Sicilian Mafia overlords were rejecting offers to take control of their Families due to Government crackdowns, Marotte could not resist the temptation in ascending to the throne of the Corsican Mob. Known as a cutthroat in all phases of Mob operations, his path was littered with corpses along his way to the top of the volcano. He was now in control of one of the most powerful factions of organized crime in Europe, and was faced with a major issue that had to be resolved this evening.

William was escorted through the massive pillars supporting the portico leading into the palatial estate overlooking the hill-covered terrain. The three men brought him to where four plainclothes armed guards led him across the marbled patio to the massive wooden doors leading to the enormous lobby area. They continued down a long carpeted hall to a great study hall that resembled the interior of a museum. It was here where Gilles Marotte awaited.

"Welcome, my friend, have a seat," Marotte came over to shake hands. He was a powerfully-built man with graying hair, steely eyes and a lantern jaw. He wore a $1,000 red satin robe and smoked with a long cigarette holder. He sat at a throne-like chair at the round table in the center of the lavishly-carpeted circular room which featured bookcases rising two stories high to a steel-framed sky dome.

"It is an honor and privilege to meet you," William smiled, gazing out at the Olympic-sized pool beyond the plate glass windows facing the breathtaking view of the moonlit landscape. "This is a wonderful place you have here."

"The rewards of a lifetime of loyalty and hard work," Marotte smiled wryly as a gigantic bodyguard arrived with a tray containing a bottle of $2,000 Spanish cognac, two glasses and a small bucket of ice. He poured the bronze liquid into the short-stemmed goblets and handed one to each man before taking his leave.

"Exquisite," William smiled after sipping from his glass. "You have excellent taste."

"A man's taste often becomes a measure of his character: the friends he chooses, the clothes he wears, the place where he lives. No matter how lofty or humble, it is important that he chooses well," Marotte spoke with a clipped French accent. "I believe one's choice of friends is the most important. Honorable men go with honorable men, do you agree?"

"Yes, most certainly."

"Your friends are somewhat enigmatic. As it's written in the Bible, they are like the wind. No one knows where they come from or where they go. This European Council of yours appears to be shrouded in secrecy. Even our highest connections in INTERPOL are unable to access the classified files on their activities. It's a level of security normally reserved for military communications."

"This is the key to our strength," William folded his hands. "Consider the fact that our network is economic in nature and our negotiations conducted entirely in cyberspace. Our membership is comprised of speculators who invest in enterprises that are not always considered legitimate by the global community. Rest assured that if our members were exposed, the shock waves would impact the nations of the world.

The benefit to you is that no one could ever prove that you had anything to do with us, because they could never prove we exist."

"So even if you were captured and tortured, there would be little that you could divulge."

"Sad but true."

"Yes, I agree," Marotte leaned back in his throne. "Of course, we are meeting here to discuss an entirely different matter. Tell me your thoughts about Emiliano Murra."

"A very capable man," William weighed his words carefully. "A man of honor. On a personal level, I found him to be quite sociable, one quite easy to do business with."

"Did you ever find any reason to think him careless in any way?"

"No, not until the details surrounding his death were made known. I believe there were many things we will never know. I think the lack of knowledge will cause the reasons behind Emiliano's death to be forever obscured."

"Did you ever discuss Enrique Chupacabra with him?"

"One thing we never discuss is opinions about business associates," William was emphatic. "When the Council decides to do business with another group, we see their representatives as being just that. To denigrate the agent is to disrespect the association. Discrepancies are reported and resolved on higher levels. I never saw any reason to give a bad report on Mr. Chupacabra."

"Yet it was you who put Emiliano together with Chupacabra. You never saw such a thing like this coming?"

"I had—heard rumors that Chupacabra might have been making deals on the side that were peripheral to the scope of our operation," William admitted. "Yet from what I understood, that was—is—the nature of the drug trade. The more money you lay at the feet of your superiors, the quicker you rise within the organization. We saw no reason to anticipate any foul play or double-cross on the part of Chupacabra, and in my opinion I do not believe Emiliano had any part in anything Chupacabra might have been involved in."

"You and your superiors are aware that one of the gold shipments had been tampered with. Tungsten bars had been substituted for gold bars that had been laundered through the Bank of Montreal by Amschel Bauer. Thanks to Bauer's wizardry, even the Mounties were unable to trace the transaction. The problem we have is that there are still people within the Colombian Cartel who suspect us of complicity in the swindle. With Bauer in prison and our trust betrayed, this grand scheme of an international crime syndicate controlling the global economy has gone up in smoke."

"As you say, we have come together to put the matter of Emiliano Murra to rest and move on to greater and bolder enterprises," William replied.

"Yes we have. I have a couple of questions."

"Certainly."

"What would cause a man like Emiliano Murra, a man who built his career on never making mistakes, to make the one fatal error that cost him his life? And, why is it that reliable sources maintain that you were the last person to see Emiliano prior to his death?"

"As I said, our philosophy is not to judge. Gossip is a cancer that has eaten away at the greatest organizations in history. In this case, I can only speculate that Chupacabra had approached Emiliano with a side deal, and they were in turn betrayed by a rival group. Of this I am sure: Chupacabra had many enemies. As far as me being the last person seen with Emiliano, that is entirely possible. He was our exclusive liaison with our organization. Had I seen him consorting with Chupacabra, I think not only I but the Colombian cartel would have been very concerned."

"Perhaps," Marotte said quietly.

"Let me ask this. All of Europe knows the reputation and the nature of the *Unione Corse*. Your organization is slow to forget an insult and quick to avenge an injury. Why would I agree to come out here to meet you if I had been involved in the death of one of your lieutenants?"

"I admire your perception," Marotte decided. "Plus, you've got balls. I like that even more. Let us put the matter of Emiliano aside for now. I want to hear your proposition."

"We want to invest in the Russian gun-running operation," William replied. "Money is no object. You know we have the resources to transport the weapons from Southern Europe to New York City, or anywhere along the American East Coast. We will go fifty-fifty on your commission with a guarantee, twenty-five percent with no guarantee."

"You are asking for a large share," Marotte sipped his cognac. "We were the ones who were transporting the bullion on your behalf for the Cartel. Now you are asking to provide the service for us."

"NATO is onto you. The Americans know it was Emiliano who arranged the transport of the bullion into Montreal. They have that super-satellite, Chernobyl, monitoring all activity crossing the Atlantic into America. They read the numbers on ships the way traffic cops check out license plates. We're your best option to get your guns across the pond."

"We are getting a quarter-mil for each shipping container. Four containers is a million dollars. If you are intercepted, you guarantee reimbursement for the loss at a rate of fifty percent."

"Fifty percent makes us partners. Twenty-five percent compensates us for the risk of having the French, or the British, or the Americans confiscating our vessel. It also puts us out of the game once INTERPOL puts the trace on our ship. Of course, if we were partners sharing fifty-fifty, perhaps our speculators would not abandon the table so easily."

"I know of you, William," Marotte grinned, pointing the cigarette holder at him. "I was one of the so-called 'godfathers' who was counselled when your European Council made their proposition. Emiliano had a high opinion of you, he said you were a shrewd negotiator and a man of respect. This is why we were so disappointed when our joint operation ended so badly."

"Negotiators cannot control what happens on the field. You should know that."

"Let me contact my associates and tell them I will endorse this deal. I will expect to hear from you through the normal channels."

The man known as William Bruce was soon on his way back to the private airstrip, where a Learjet 85 Bombardier would return him to Southern France. He had succeeded in his mission and would now wait and see where the next chapter in the relationship between the *Corse Unione* and the European Council would take him.

Chapter Two

Colonel Mark O'Shaughnessy awaited his guests at the SIS Building at Vauxhall Cross on 85 Albert Embankment that next morning. He was mildly piqued that the operation seemed to have been thrown together so haphazardly. Yet he knew that developments on the world scene had dictated their timetable, and once again the safety of the free world was dropped in his lap. He also knew that he was but a cog in the vast machine, but his superiors were not providing him the luxury of allowing him to think so.

He had worked with two of the operatives before, and though they made a dynamic team he wondered whether they could reconcile their differences once again. Though they had continued to work deep undercover, they were different as night and day in every perspective. The third person was an unknown factor. He had been given a sizeable dossier but it still did not tell him who the real person was. Hopefully this meeting would improve his vision.

"Well, not that everyone's here, let the meeting begin. You two gentlemen know each other, but out of respect for our newest member of the team, let us introduce ourselves. I am Colonel Mark O'Shaughnessy, formerly of the SAS and currently with MI6."

"I'm Captain William Shanahan, formerly of the SAS and currently with MI6," the man known as William Bruce said curtly.

"You wanna go, then?" the next man grinned.

"Please," O'Shaughnessy urged him.

"Aw reet. I'm John Oliver Cromwell Gawain, my friends call me Jack. I'm working under the auspices of the Special Reconnaissance Regiment with the Narcotics Division of the PSNI[1]."

William did a double-take, a dumbfounded look on his face. It forced both Mark and Jack to suppress a smile.

"I am Special Agent Lucretia Carcosa. I report directly to the Director of INTERPOL, and I am the leader of a Joint Investigation Team which will be coordinating activities with me on this particular assignment."

"Well, they're hiring 'em young and good-lookin' these days, I can see," Gawain leaned back in his chair.

"A bit of decorum will do here, Gawain," Mark advised him.

"Don't hold your breath," William muttered.

"From one and all," Mark stared at William, who looked away. "Let's get down to business, shall we?"

"Aye, I've got a feelin' this may take a while," Jack added.

"I'm sure everyone is aware of the political situation in the Ukraine," Mark began. "The Russian annexation of the Crimea has created a military crisis in the region. In response to NATO sanctions against the Federation, the Russians have deployed Special Forces units throughout Eastern Europe. The Americans believe they are negotiating with the Russian Mob and Chechen terror groups to possibly coordinate strikes in the US and the UK. They believe these NATO sanctions may threaten the political stability of the Federation."

"What political stability?" Jack smirked. "Ever hear of Pussy Riot?"

"Whether it's an excuse to retaliate against NATO is a moot point," Mark continued. "The fact remains that INTERPOL has determined there is a gun-running operation being planned to ship weapons from the Ukraine into Poland, through Germany into France. From there they plan to move the armaments across the Atlantic into the East Coast of the US. These weapons will be used by terror groups to stage

---

1. Police Services of Northern Ireland

operations across the country, particularly in New York City. The theory is that they can plunge the City into a state of martial law and paralyze the Western economy in doing so."

"Do we have proof that these things are in progress, or is this speculation?" William asked.

"If I may, Colonel," Lucretia rose from her seat.

"Certainly, Agent Carcosa."

She was a beautiful woman with long black hair that reached halfway down her back, her lovely features enhanced by sky-blue eyes and ruby lips. She stood 5'9" and had a long-legged hourglass figure. She spoke with a French accent that reminded William of Gilles Marotte's Corsican intonation.

"INTERPOL has initiated operations in the three countries the Colonel mentioned," Lucretia expertly switched on the PC by the wall of the barren room, which activated the plasma screen on the far wall. "Operation Lublin and Operation Berlin have confirmed rumors of the gun-running activity. Our team under Colonel O'Shaughnessy will be coordinating activities with my own team under Operation Toulouse. We have determined that the smugglers are working with the criminal underworld in Western Europe to move the weapons across the Atlantic. Unfortunately, the trail grows cold outside of Toulouse, and our mission is to find out who is moving the guns out of France and to where."

"Thank you, Special Agent," O'Shaughnessy rose as he returned to her seat. Both William and Jack peered furtively at her perfectly-chiseled legs enhanced by her power dress suit.

"As you can see on the map, we see three options for the smugglers to consider. If they contract the Sicilian Mafia in Italy, there is a possibility of either shipping through the Mediterranean or going with the Irish Mob in Ireland or the Basque Militants in Spain. This appears to be the long route but the most feasible. It makes the network even harder to trace and forces us to divert more of our resources. Special Agent Carcosa will be in charge of infiltrating the Sicilian Mob in coordination with INTERPOL teams in Italy."

"Sir, do you think that may be a risky proposition for a woman, to say the least?" William wondered.

"You'll have enough to worry about on your end," Mark replied. "Agent Shanahan has successfully reestablished ties with the *Unione Corse*, the Corsican Mob. Once again we will be using our European Council cover to throw the Corsicans off-track. Shanahan, along with Carcosa, will be working to create competition between the Sicilians and the Corsicans. If it escalates into a gang war, then the Russians will have no choice but to rely on the third option."

"Why am I getting the feeling that this is where Jack comes in?" Gawain smiled.

"You've got it," Mark nodded. "Agent Gawain will be infiltrating a group known only as the Citadel. They are a band of mercenaries who hire out to the highest bidders. Up to now, we've heard rumors that they have done work for the Sicilians and the Corsicans, but we have no idea of what or where. Our concern is that if either of the Mobs are incapacitated by our operations, they might reach out to the Citadel. If they do so, Gawain would be the only source of information available to us."

"And how am I supposed to pull this off if I can't speak a word of French?"

"All three of you will have carefully constructed alibis, and you will be given Internet access to MI6 databases in order to access your individual background information. As you know, your lives may depend on this info, so you are well-advised to study it carefully. We will be sharing further information as it develops, and we will remain in constant communication with each of you. Hopefully we will be coordinating activity as the operation begins to bear fruit, and you will be given status updates on a regular basis."

"So that's it, then, hi and bye?" Jack asked. "Not even time to share a pint?"

"No, I wouldn't say that would be inappropriate," Mark replied. "As a matter of fact, since you may be placing your lives in each other's hands at one time or another during this operation, it may not be a bad idea. Ma'am, gentlemen, we will be in touch."

"I say we let William drive, he knows the area."

"Sounds good," Lucretia agreed as they took the elevator down to the parking area.

"Do you visit London much, Lucretia?" William asked as his alarm helped locate his Continental VT G-8.

"Once in a while. You can call me Luci. How about Mamuska's at the Elephant and Castle Center?"

"Sounds good."

The agents soon arrived at the mall and found a corner table where they ordered drinks and appetizers. William wore a tan suit with matching tie, meticulous with his buzzcut blond hair. Jack wore a black leather, dark jeans and Doc Martens, every bit the opposite of his ex-partner. Luci sat between them, sipping her French 75 cocktail. Jack had a Guinness and William had a vodka martini which he freely admitted was a tribute to James Bond.

"So, is all that true about you going back inside with the Unione?" Jack asked.

"Sure is. There was the thing about Murra, you remember that. I had to smooth it over with one of their top guys over drinks, but I'm a friend of a friend in good standing. What've you been up to?"

"Did either of you hear about that jackpot up on the A1 near Newry?"

"Yes, it was all over the telly," William replied.

"Well, I was in the midst of it."

"*What*?" they asked.

"Aye, we were ridin' with a meth gang from Dublin that was tryin' t' cut a deal with a crew up north. They made us somehow an' were gonna take us out, but we attracted the attention of some bikers. I shot the finger at 'em and they forced us over. There was a shootout and both sides got their backsides kicked in. My partner Danny had a hideout and tried to force the survivors t'pull over when we got rollin' again, but they drew on him and that pretty well did it. Hear tell it was a large amount of product we were drivin' around with."

"The reports said ten men were killed," Luci noted. "It must have been quite an experience."

"Speaking of experiences," Jack grinned. "What was it that qualified you to go running with the likes of us?"

"Mmm, the *golabki*," she thanked the waitress as her cabbage rolls were brought over. "I do miss it."

"This is Polish food, isn't it?" William double-checked the menu.

"Yes," she took a bite of one of the rolls. "You were asking me what my experience was."

"I believe we did," Jack drained his glass as the waitress went for another one.

"Do you remember that jackpot, as you call it, that O'Shaughnessy mentioned in Lublin?"

"He did mention something about an Operation Lublin."

"I recall something about a shootout in which an undercover team of Polish narcotics detectives were executed by the Polish Mob just before INTERPOL agents arrived," William spoke up. "The newspapers made it sound like a drug bust. How did your team get involved?"

"The Russian Mob made a deal with the Pruszkow Mafia to trade crystal meth for guns," she revealed. "I was inserted into a street gang that was dealing meth after Andrzej Kolikowski was killed in '99 and the heroin market imploded. We were contacted by the Russians and told they would do a straight-up trade. When we went in, we found out the Russians didn't bring the guns. Their plan was to rob us for the meth. One of our guys was wearing a wire, but when the detectives moved in they got ambushed. By the time our INTERPOL team arrived at the rendezvous, the Russians had escaped and I was the only survivor."

"Found a safe spot, did ye?" Jack grinned, sipping his Guinness.

"Not so safe," she pushed her seat back, pulling up her white blouse and showing them a bullet scar on the left side of her midsection. "The bullet nicked my kidney but didn't do anything serious. I suppose the fellow who took the shot figured I was done, but he didn't have a lot of time to put one in my head. It turned into a real shootout."

It was an overcast night in Pruszkow in central Poland, and the farm property located five miles outside of town was well secluded off a long dirt road off the E30 West. The road led into a heavily-wooded area with its canopied treeline making aerial surveillance impossible. It had belonged to the friend of a gang member and was used for short-term storage and as a rendezvous point as necessary. This evening there would be a meeting that was to be conducted as quickly and quietly as possible.

She had opened a curio shop in downtown Pruszkow and eventually was approached by a street dealer who asked if she was looking to make some extra money. She told him she had experience on the black market and would be interested in moving merchandise using the shop as a cover. They started off at first with the dealer conducting a couple of transactions in the back area of the store, then escalated to a transport of five kilos of heroin into an exclusive area near the Gasin District in the store's delivery van. At length she was invited to a meeting with the gang leader at the Kawiarnia Pawilon, a popular downtown coffee house.

"We have a situation on our hands," the leader advised her as they sat in a corner booth, guarded by three gunmen in the same fashion the Irish gangsters would cordon off Jack Gawain's table almost a year later. "We have gotten an offer from the Russian Mob. They are wanting to trade guns for meth, and they are talking five kilos. They have a contact who will be willing to buy the guns from us for a good price. This can be a game-changer for us. They will be buying out our available stock, but with the resale of the guns we will be able to open up a second lab. What we need is a driver and another gunslinger at the meeting. We are equal-opportunity employers, you see. We would just as soon have you come along with us as we would have a faggot, or a nigger. If this works well, we could bring you in as a full partner."

"I hope you're not looking at me like a faggot or a nigger."

"Not at all. I think you're very attractive. You must bear in mind that our competitors and clients may have a different outlook."

"Okay, I'm in. I'll just have to earn respect like everyone else."

"You've earned mine. That's a start."

And so it was that the newest gang member was at the wheel as the minivan cruised down the highway and bumped its way along the dirt road to the worn-down farm property off the E-30. She had three of the gang members with her, the leader sitting alongside her and two behind her guarding a satchel containing the five kilos of meth. The leader and his top gun had Uzis under their trenchcoats, while everyone else including her carried Glocks. They spotted another minivan parked in front of the barn where the meeting was scheduled. They parked alongside it, satisfied that the area appeared to be otherwise deserted.

The leader did his job, leading the way into the darkened barn. Dimly illuminated by battery-operated lanterns, there was a long table set by the wall to the right here four chairs were set on either side. As was planned, the Uzi man and the satchel-bearer stood on either side of the entrance as the others approached the table. Four Russians stepped forth from the far wall and took their seats.

"You bring your girlfriend to a business meeting?" the Russian leader spoke Polish with a thick accent.

"This is not my girlfriend, this is our partner."

"It makes me question your judgment. If she were to be arrested and the authorities come looking for us, rest assured there would be more lives endangered than those in this room."

"We came to do business, not to exchange idle threats. If you had that kind of power you wouldn't need us."

"Think of the kind of men who are able to take possession of such weapons as these and bring them across the Ukraine with impunity," the leader stared at the Pole menacingly. "They are the same kind of men who overthrew the Crimean government without any backup from the Russian Army. They would have no problem coming in here to avenge a double-cross. What we do have a problem with is crossing into Germany speaking Polish as a second language."

"Let's quit talking bullshit and get down to business. I don't see the guns in this room."

"I see a man standing by the door with a satchel beside him. Tell him to bring it to the table and allow us to sample what you've brought."

"You've already had your sample. Look, I thought this was a done deal. We screw you over, you know where to find us. This is not a fly-by-night operation, you know that."

"We need to see the product."

The leader crooked his finger and the gangster at the door picked up the satchel. He brought it to the table and was about to hoist it up.

"Set it on the ground, and open it so I can see it."

The gangster put it back down, and as soon as he reached for the straps, a hollow-point bullet penetrated the top of his head. It was a routine deception, focusing everyone's attention on the satchel so that the shooter could got the drop on everyone else.

She remembered the impact of the bullet slamming into her mid-section, and recoiling from the impact, and eventually the INTERPOL team swooping in. She was transported to a hospital in Warsaw, and eventually flown from Berlin to Paris.

The woman from the curio shop in Pruszkow was never heard from again.

Chapter Three

A week later, the man called William Bruce took a flight to Paris International Airport and checked into the Hotel Four Seasons George V. It was conveniently located near the Champs-Elysees where his meeting was scheduled to take place. He opted to have dinner in his room so as to support the storyline of the European Council being a phantasmal enigma. It was somewhat of an inconvenience as he had not been in Paris for a few years and would have liked to enjoy the downtown ambiance. Regardless, the job came first, and in this case it could eventually become a matter of life and death.

He arrived at Le Showcase, a jet-set favorite on the hallowed boulevard whose surreal décor attracted politicians and celebrities from around the world. Gilles Marotte had reserved tables in the lounge, a pink-lit area lined by double rows of alcove walls and electric flame strips. Pairs of gunmen sat on either side of the table reserved for Marotte, and he stood to greet William as the waitress brought an iced bucket of Moet et Chandon.

"I am pleased to announce that my associates are looking forward to join with the Council in this project," Marotte said once the waitress poured their glasses before departing. "There seems to be only one fly in the ointment. The Russians are also contracting with the Italians to have the guns transported. Apparently they are wanting to see who is more efficient in handling the job. It seems that the Russian President is escalating his efforts to destabilize the Ukrainian government. He is greatly concerned over attempts by NATO to retaliate. If they launch a campaign of retaliation, he wants the weapons to be in the hands of the extremists without delay."

"So this is something that would happen within the next few weeks," William sipped his champagne.

"Weeks, months, years, who can say? You know how things are in the political world. They say the world is on the brink of war, then the following week they say they have reached an agreement. Only the people in the hot spot realize things are worse than ever. The Russians' angle is that ethnic Russians' lives are being threatened in the Ukraine. If the Government is powerless to act, the extremists will instigate a civil war so the Federation can send in its troops. Should NATO begin deploying, the terrorists in the US and the UK will launch their attacks. The Americans and the British will be too busy at home to compromise themselves overseas."

"If we're shipping directly from the French coast, we should have an advantage in shipping time," William reasoned. "It should take the competition an extra day to ship from the Mediterranean and circle the Spanish coast."

"The problem we have are these newcomers, the Citadel. Somehow they made contact with the Russians and want to deal into the game. The Russians don't have enough information about them and are reluctant to negotiate. They have made contact with our people and told us they can take the Italians out of the picture. Of course, such a thing could cause a gang war that would paralyze both sides. We believe that this would provide them the subterfuge they would need to swipe the deal right out from our noses."

"What do we know about these people?"

"Less than we know about your organization," Marotte smiled wryly. "Our contacts in INTERPOL have almost nothing on them. There are rumors that they have hired out as mercenaries in civil wars around the globe and have trained insurgent forces throughout Africa and the Middle East. They are also suspected of drug smuggling and kidnappings in South America, but of course no one has made positive identification. They enforce secrecy through terror and murder, and it seems to work very well for them."

"Let me ask you something," William confided. "Have you picked up anything on a mid-level gunman called Jack Gain?"

"No, should I have heard of him?"

"I'm not sure. He hired out to us last year during the Operation Blackout. He was with me a couple of times when I met with Emiliano Murra. His backstory was that he was a captain with a UDA[1] splinter group. After the project ended, we heard rumors that Gain had assassinated someone for MI6 to earn his parole. The last we heard, he was sighted in the Basque regions of Spain. Now, either he's going political with the Basque separatists, or he's building currency to make a connection across the sea."

"If he's not talking to the Sicilians, and he hasn't come to us…"

"Precisely. He left us without notice, and he's hiding himself very well. I'm wondering if he's trying to make contact with this Citadel."

"I can spread the word," Marotte decided. "Should we be concerned?"

"He might be considered a triple-threat. He's a serial killer and a mass murderer, and our psychological analysts conclude that he could easily turn suicide bomber if threatened. We're not certain as to his motivations or if he has any allegiances. I'm thinking he may be useful as a double agent if he is trying to enlist in the Citadel."

"Curious," Marotte cocked an eyebrow. "If he gets connected with the Basque, they may be very interested in a weapons deal of their own. It also gives him a shipping port on the Atlantic which he could use to bargain with this Citadel."

"Perhaps your people can keep an eye out for him. We are also trying to find out what he is up to. We think he may be useful. If not, we may be able to convince him to remain on the sidelines – one way or another."

"You seem to hold him in high regard."

---

1. Ulster Defense Association

"I've worked with him," William assured Marotte. "He is a very capable man."

The man known as Jack Gain was not yet a topic of discussion in a conversation held hours earlier in a place hundreds of miles from the Champs-Elysees. Don Cesare Masseroli was a well-respected godfather in the Sicilian Mob, owning a vineyard and an olive garden on his palatial estate in the suburb of Montelepre in Palermo from where he ruled his fiefdom with an iron hand. Though semi-retired due to his losing battle with lung cancer, Masseroli was still a valued advisor to the Mob and acted as a consultant and analyst for his fellow bosses.

Don Cesare had lunch served on the patio overlooking his botanical garden, which extended fifty yards south to the rear of the mansion. He had a shrimp salad served along with a side dish lasagna and a platter of veal parmigiana with angel hair pasta. The Don practiced the ancient custom of having different cuisines served at meals, with guests encouraged to take only a couple of bites to save room for all the other food to be sampled. Leftovers were either thrown to the dogs or sent to peasants in the nearby village.

"Bread and olive oil, wine and cheese, that is what the meal is all about," Don Cesare toasted his guest with a glass of chianti. "Everything else is appetizer. Of those four things, we here in Sicily enjoy the best."

"I cannot disagree with you," the woman known as Lucinda Montesano savored her wine. "This is excellent. You make your own wine here, do you not?"

"As well as the oil, the bread and the cheese, this is why I brag," Cesare chuckled. "What of you, my dear? I've heard nothing but good things about you. I understand you were working with the Polish Mob in Pruszkow. That was a very unfortunate situation, how things ended there."

"Yes, it appeared there was an informant in our midst. Someone tipped off the Policja[2] and they had the place entirely surrounded. Some of us tried to escape through a side exit but they opened fire on us. I was hit in the side and had to be flown to Warsaw. Fortunately my connections were able to help me escape from the Warsaw Medical Center. All the police got was my fingerprints and a fictitious name. My connections also torched the curio shop that night, leaving no trace of me behind."

"Very efficient. We have all the respect in the world for the Poles. Their country is the gateway for drug trafficking in Europe, and they fight hard to protect their ground just as their forefathers did during World War II. Sometimes the Russians and the Germans think their land is but a Polish corridor. The Poles always find a way to make them see otherwise."

"Yes, that's true."

"So you believe this curio store front will work again?"

"There's no reason why it should not. The Policja never made a connection between me and the store. The insurance claim was handled entirely by Internet. The only ones who know I ever existed was the Polish Mob. This is why they feel I am the best candidate to make this happen. With my trucks, I can transport the guns from Poland to Germany, across the Alps into Italy. We can establish connections with trading companies and museums along the route which will throw the police and INTERPOL off entirely. We consider this a foolproof plan."

"I particularly like the idea of crossing the Alps. That will make it virtually impossible for hijackers to intercept shipments leaving Germany. There would be too great a threat of being detected by the Swiss or the Austrians. If you are certain your people could guarantee passage through Germany, I don't see why this could not work."

"The Polish Mob has a number of strong contacts throughout Germany. As you know, there is no German Mob in the traditional sense of the term. The German underworld is comprised largely of large

2. National Police

gangs that form a large cooperative network. Our major connections are with the Heisenberg Gang in Berlin and the Sjoberg Gang in Munich. The Sjobergs are very influential in Southern Germany. I would venture to say it will be the safest area on our route."

"If this works out, I see no reason why we could not plan on having the route working both ways. We have regular shipments of cocaine from Colombia coming into the Mediterranean, as well as heroin coming in from the Golden Triangle on Asia. You can become an integral part of this network."

"I would be very much looking forward to it. We anticipate the Sicilian-Polish connection to be most profitable to all of us in time to come."

It was a couple of weeks later when the man known as Jack Gain began making his own connections in Southern France. He arrived in Toulouse days after the briefing in London, quickly setting up shop and raising his flag. He flew from London to the Toulouse-Blagnac International Airport, then rented out a car and cruised over to the Ville Rose. He rented a room at the Hotel de France before heading over to The Frog and Rosbif. It was an English-themed pub, and the bartender was glad to have someone from the Old Country to talk to. Jack began stopping in for lunch and soon made casual acquaintances with most of the regulars. He also stopped in at different hours during the evening and bought drinks for those he grew to recognize.

He arranged for Six to call every other day through an MI6 switch, which would be a heads-up for any underworld figure. They would know that Jack was using the pub to forward messages so as to avoid satellite traces as well as hanging his shingle. Once he got that going, he made it a point to sit at the bar and study the rugby betting statistics. It let people know he was a gambling man. He would also go outside for a cigarette break or two, making himself a familiar figure on the Rue de l'Industrie.

Six and his logistical team was also establishing a phony network, sending double agents into the Toulouse-Blagnac area and making deals with low-level hoods. They, in turn, made mention of the fact to their superiors. The gangsters were quick to notice the incursion of wiseguys with British connections. They spread the word that they wanted to have a sitdown, and it did not take long for one of their people to approach Jack Gain.

"You from England?" a short, stocky man dressed in a black suit, charcoal suit and silvery tie sidled up to him one morning before noon.

"Aye, in and around, y'might say. Who wants to know?"

"I do. Do you bet on the horses?"

"Let's just say I do better with the horses than with rugby."

"The usual, Mr. H?" the bartender, John Falstaff, came over.

"Yeah, sure," he replied. He had thinning black hair, narrow dark eyes and a cruel mouth. Jack knew that a physical altercation would turn into a fight to the finish. "You know anyone at Kempton Park?"

"A couple of guys. I spend more time at Sandown Park. More stuff goin' on there."

"Like what?"

"Hip-hop concerts, shite like that. Why, you do vendors booths?"

"*Merde*," he growled. "Do I look like I work out of vendors' booths?"

"There's nothin' wrong with it, fella. A few thousand pounds for a few hours work. Plus there's a lot more ye can sell than T-shirts and CD's if you got the right stuff."

"So you got the right stuff?" he spoke with a thick Corsican accent.

"Lots of people in London think so."

"Why don't we go outside and have a smoke? Maybe you can tell me something about your stuff."

Jack followed him out, and they walked down the block to where the man's Citroen C4 Cactus was parked.

"And what does the H stand for?"

"Hornec. Jean-Paul Hornec."

"Jack Gain. Pleased t'meet ye."

"Let's sit in the car so we can have some privacy."

"Sounds good to me."

They hopped inside the luxury car as Jack accepted one of his Gitanes cigarettes. Jack gave him a light and they blew smoke out the windows, savoring the rich tobacco.

"So who do you know at the track? You got inside connections?"

"Yeah, I know some guys. We only do fixes once in a blue moon t'throw off the Horseracing Authority. Plus if ye bet heavy ye'll have to have th' money comin' from inside th' border. Otherwise if ye win, they're almost sure to investigate."

"I'm not talking about placing bets. I mean connections inside the stables."

"Aye, well, what're ye lookin' for?"

"We need someone who's in with the veterinary staff. Someone who's got access to the medicine."

"I think I can hook you up with somethin'. What've ye got in mind?"

"Are you a cop?"

"Piss off. Are you?"

"All right, my friend," Jean-Paul glanced at him before returning his gaze to a woman walking up the street. "We're looking to buy some Xylazine. It's a horse sedative."

"Aye, I know what it is. Ye got a cook?"

"You don't need to know that."

"Aw reet. Do ye have anyone in the UK to move the dope for ye?"

"You don't need to know that either."

"Well, look here, fellow," Jack peered over at him. "My people aren't gonna be good with movin' horse tranquilizer across the Channel for chicken feed. If we get it to you, we'd want to be able t'bring some back."

"I'm not sure your people want that kind of heat, my friend. It turns junkies into zombies. When the bobbies see them staggering around the streets of London, they'll tear up the streets looking for you."

"Never shite in yer own back yard. I know your people aren't sellin' the shite in front of the Eiffel Tower."

"Okay, I'll talk to my people, I'll run some numbers by you."

"Mr. H," Jack smirked. "Quite an inside joke, I'd say."

"Quite. You need to keep in mind that we've got heavy connections along the Mediterranean. If we catch any heat on your end, we'll cut you off immediately. We can't risk anything coming back on our suppliers."

"No problem. By the way, my people are gonna want t'know who they're dealing with."

"You tell them they are dealing with me."

"C'mon, give me a break. Yer gonna need t'know who I'm with."

"My cousins are the leaders of the Hornec Gang in Montreuil."

"Aye, but that's not who you're with."

"If I give you numbers, I'll need to bring you to meet the man who will back the numbers."

"So that's the one who I'll be doin' business with."

"I'll meet you here same time tomorrow," he switched on the ignition.

"Sounds good."

Jack exited the vehicle and headed back inside. He felt very much like a fisherman who just made his first big catch.

Chapter Four

That next evening, William Shanahan checked into the Crowne Plaza Toulouse after arriving at the airport and renting a vehicle for transportation. Located within walking distance of the Ville Rose, he decided that it was a prime location to operate from. He would be awaiting contact with the Corsicans as they made arrangements to finalize their deal with the Russian Mob. The newscasts were ablaze with bulletins over civil unrest throughout Eastern Europe, and it looked like the Russians were going to make a move any time soon. The European Council would be expected to hold up their end of the bargain once the agreement was reached.

He knew that Jack has arrived in Toulouse several days ago. Six had given William indication that Jack was on the move, so chances were slim that they would run into one another. He had no idea what Lucinda was up to. He had not grown comfortable with the idea of working with a woman on the team in a field position. Yet he was sure that she would be able to hold her own. He grimaced at the memory of women soldiers who had been wounded in combat in Iraq and Afghanistan. No matter how battle-hardened a trooper might be, the sight of a woman or child hit by gunfire was something one would never forget.

He took his morning shower and began sorting out his clothes for the day when he heard the chimes sounding on his cell phone. His heart warmed when he saw it was Morgana Mc Laren. He spent his last night in London on the phone with his fiancée, and was greatly looking forward to the upcoming wedding next year on Easter Sunday. They had scheduled it well in advance, so it would take something on the level of World War III for him to cancel his plans.

"Good morning, darling. How're you doing?"

"Just wonderful. I've got some great news."

"Oh, and what's that, precious?"

"Fianna and I are going to be able to fly out to Toulouse for a week."

"*What*?"

"Oh, I know you're out there on business, but we'll stay out of your way. You know Fianna had gotten her job back with the airline, and they gave her accumulated time back. We talked to one of the managers, and he pulled some strings so we could fly out together. I figured she could keep me company while you were buys. We were really hoping that Jack might be working with you again."

His head was spinning as he tried to collect his thoughts. He could not believe what he was hearing.

"How—how did you find out where I was?"

"Well, you remember that friend of mine in Homeland Security? I asked her for a favor. I hope you're not upset. It's just that we haven't seen each other for weeks, and I've never been to Toulouse. It sounded like such a romantic place to meet."

"I'm in the midst of some deep stuff, love. The same sort as last time. My immediate concern would having you placed in danger."

"Well, rest assured I'm not going to be following you around golf courses at midnight. I'll be at my hotel room, you'll know where to find me, and hopefully we'll be able to spend some time together before either one of us has to leave."

He could tell by the tone in her voice that she was not going to be put off. She was coming to Toulouse come hell or high water.

"All right. But you can't call me here, and you can't come looking for me. I'll call you. I have no way of telling whether my calls are being monitored by satellite. I wouldn't know if I'm under surveillance. You know what kind of business I'm involved in. You have to promise me."

"Don't worry, darling. I'll send you a text if I want you to call me. I'll just leave my initials, no message. If you call me, just use a pay phone. That sounds pretty James Bond foolproof to me."

"I'm not comfortable with this, Morgana. I'm not here for relaxation."

"I'll be about my own business, and you tend to yours. If you have some spare time, we'll get together for dinner. Maybe we can go fool around afterwards."

When he clicked off, he stared out the picture window for a long while. He could not believe something like this was happening. He had trusted Morgana with his life before. She was the one who stitched him up after the gunfight with Murra and Chupacabra last year. Yet Fianna Hesher was somewhat of a loose cannon, Jack Gawain's perfect counterpart. If she were to come around looking for Jack, it could easily blow their cover. He realized he would have to deal with it as things developed. There was no point in worrying about it now.

The fact that Homeland Security could trace an MI6 agent with impunity was a cause of great concern. If an airline stewardess was able to call in a marker with an ex-colleague for that kind of information, how much more could an extortionist with a major criminal organization gain access to? He knew that the US satellite Chernobyl had the ability to locate a fly on a horse's arse given its coordinates anywhere on the planet. Yet no one knew who had access to its technology or its information. It was an unsettling thought, but nothing worth worrying about. He had a job to do, and distraction on the field was one sure way to get yourself killed.

He heard the chimes going off again as he finished dressing, and for a strange moment he hoped it was Morgana. He was astonished at himself on how hard he had fallen for that woman. He retrieved his phone from the desk in the spacious living room and saw it was one of the Corsicans. They had a prearranged code of VSOP on their Caller ID, after the cognac brand that Gilles Marotte preferred.

"This is Rene Chatillon," the voice answered. "Meet me at L'Autre Salon in a half hour. I will be wearing a dark blue suit and rose-colored glasses."

William dutifully began tidying up and going down his mental checklist before heading to the hotel lobby. He was mildly irritated because he wanted to find a local gym and catch a quick workout. He knew there were plenty of places to go running, as France was one of the foremost nations of joggers in Europe. Still, he stuck to a diligent workout regimen and tried to hit the weights at least three times a week. He felt as if he had settled down in a city when he found a good gym, and would make it a priority once he got his meet-and-greet with the Corsicans out of the way.

Chatillon was a tall, well-built man about William's height of six foot-one, though about twenty pounds lighter. They shook hands as Chatillon discarded his cigarette before they entered the coffee house. William knew that the man following them from behind was with the other two well-dressed men standing by a car parked at the curb out front. Obviously Chatillon was a man of respect among his Corsican peers.

"It's nice when you can mix business with pleasure," Chatillon thanked the waitress for a menu. "Toulouse is one of my favorite cities. I haven't been here for quite a while."

"Very nice. I saw all the pink tiles on the rooftops from the plane window. It certainly does appear as a Pink City."

"Yes, quite lovely. Hopefully we will wrap up our business dealings in a short time and be able to enjoy some of the nightlife while we're here."

Chatillon ordered a tulipe with raspberry sorbet while William settled for an apricot-almond clafouti. He would have preferred a regular breakfast but enjoyed the pastry nonetheless.

"History books depict Marie Antoinette most unfavorably in her response to the crowds rioting in the streets for bread. 'Let them eat cake', she said. I don't think most foreigners would have thought that a bad idea," Chatillon smiled as he wiped his fingers with a napkin.

"Certainly not worth losing one's head over," William agreed.

"It appears we may have reached a deal with the competition," Chatillon revealed. "The Russians have struck a deal with the Polish Mob and the Sjoberg Gang to have the shipment delivered to the Italian border. They will transport the items to Grenoble, where our people will bring it across France to the coast of Bretagne. From there we will expect your organization to take possession and complete the transaction in New York."

"Excellent. When and where should we expect to accept the delivery?"

"We will keep you posted. The shipment should arrive in the province within forty-eight hours. You will be given at least twenty-four notice as to where the final destination is scheduled. Would that be sufficient?"

"I don't anticipate a problem," William sipped his Colombian coffee.

"Good," Chatillon smiled. "Do you have plans for this evening?"

"No, not really."

"We've been told that Les Coulisses is quite an enjoyable place to relax. It is located on Strasbourg Boulevard, we've already made reservations. I'll give you a call around eight this evening."

"Sounds like a great idea. I'll look forward to hearing from you."

William and Chatillon parted ways outside the restaurant shortly afterward. William made his way back to the hotel to contact Six. They would have to find a way to ensure that the arms shipment would never make it to Bretagne.

The woman known as Lucinda Montesano took a red-eye flight from Palermo to Milan for a meeting with Giovanni Cusimano, widely recognized as the godfather of the province of Venezia. Cusimano and Masseroli had done business for nearly half a century and had made millions of dollars arranging transport of contraband across the Alps into Northern Italy. Don Giovanni was as taken aback as Don Cesare upon learning that their newest partner was a woman, but deferred to the recommendations of his associates in welcoming her to his mansion.

It was a Mediterranean-style residence set on twenty acres of landscaped property with its own orchards, vineyards and olive gardens. Overlooking Lake Como just an hour's drive from Milan, the snow-capped mountain ranges in the distance provided a breathtaking view. The grounds were so captivating that it was often included on sight-seeing tours from Milan. Cusimano employed a dozen maids and gardeners along with a twelve-man squad of bodyguards to maintain around-the-clock vigilance over the estate.

"I'm pleased to announce that the initial transaction will be conducted within the next twenty-four hours," Cusimano revealed as they sat on the patio at the rear of the house on the second level overlooking the picturesque landscape. "We will send the location of the rendezvous point to the website you've been provided. We will call your cell phone and give you the website address. You will have an hour to access the information before we close the website. If you are unable to get online for whatever reason, we will give you an alternate site. It ensures that the police have no way to intercept the message."

"It's encouraging to know your organization is so thorough," Lucinda raised her glass of chianti to him. "The way things are these days, there is no telling whether any country on earth would hesitate to have detainees sent to Guantanamo Bay. The American Government would leap at the opportunity to send anyone there if they could be implicated in a terror threat."

"Yes, the stakes have gotten much higher, and this is why we are able to pay more. Twenty five thousand to bring a container full of weapons across Liechtenstein. Bank robbers do well to come away with that much in this day and age."

"Perhaps skinheads covered with tattoos going in like a suicide squad in broad daylight," she gave a throaty laugh. "I think my target would be the armored truck."

"And how would you handle that?"

"Oh, I don't know. Two vehicles, one blocking, the second one attacking form the rear. The front vehicle would use a concussion grenade to take out the windshield, then a gas grenade to take out the guards. An explosive to break the lock on the rear door, not powerful enough to damage the money. With enough rehearsal, it could be done in ten minutes or less."

"For argument's sake, suppose they fought back?"

"An armor-piercing grenade would end it. You would probably destroy some of the money, but something is better than nothing."

"There is much that I like about you," Cusimano squeezed a slice of lemon into his demitasse. Like everything else, he merely sampled the wine and left most of the glass to be taken away. "Being a very beautiful woman is beside the point. I'll have you know you are the only woman who has come here in this capacity. Some of the most powerful men in Europe have sat in the seat where you are, but never a woman."

"I am truly honored, Don Giovanni."

"Tell me about the incident in Pruszkow," he stared into her eyes. "I've heard the police version and I've heard the Poles' version. I would like to hear it from you."

"There's not a whole lot to tell, unfortunately," she buttered a slice of Italian bread and dipped it into the small dish of olive oil next to her salad plate. "Apparently the Russians had been intercepted by the Policja at some point, and they were substituted by undercover detectives. They must have been authentic because I would have caught their accents had they been Poles speaking Russian. I suspected something when they did not immediately produce the weapons. That would have been the correct procedure for a visiting group in foreign territory. Yet there was the possibility that they had left the guns outside in case there was a police raid. They played the sting perfectly."

"You were the only survivor. You were the first one to take a bullet."

"It probably saved my life, and cost my friend Jurczak his. When the detectives announced themselves, I went to draw my weapon but the Poles had the drop on us. They opened fire and Jurczak shoved me down when I got hit. He sacrificed his life to protect me."

"And, of course, the Policja announced that the Russians got away with the heroin," Cusimano shook his head. "It allowed them to keep the case open on the Russian smugglers, plus god only knows what they did with the drugs."

"It also made them look like heroes for gunning down my confederates," she said with a tinge of emotion. "I found it interesting that they never mentioned my arrest nor my escape in the newspapers. It seems the Polish government exercises more control over the press than other nations in the EU. Of course, that is how it should be."

"Which makes it harder for people like you and I to make a living," he chuckled, gesturing toward her. "*Te salut, senorita.*"

"People like you and I should never be in the papers," she said before taking a bite of her bread. "It is a mistake I managed to avoid and do not intend to repeat."

"Spoken like a true professional. I am sure you won't."

"So I'll be coming through Liechtenstein?"

"Would you prefer Switzerland or Austria?"

"The shortest path between two points is a straight line."

All she had to figure out was how to ensure the shipment would never reach Italy without becoming a murder victim in the aftermath.

That evening, the man known as William Bruce arrived at Les Coulisses. The ultra-modern nightclub was bathed in soft pastels, its futuristic ambiance making it the place to be on a Saturday evening. They were playing the latest dub music, and couples were already on the dance floor despite the fact it was only 9 PM. He strolled out to the patio and saw Rene Chatillon along with the four men seated two at a table on either side of his corner spot.

"William, how good to see you," Chatillon rose to shake hands. "It is good that we are meeting at this time. In a couple of hours it will be wall-to-wall people."

"I'm an early riser myself. I just came out to have a drink and see what this place was like."

"I agree, I'm not the party person I used to be. After a while it becomes all part of the endless stream of women, wine and song. Although one never gets tired of it, or at least we hope to never reach that stage."

There was a bottle on Moet et Chandon on ice in a bucket, and Chatillon poured them both a glass before they toasted each other and sipped their champagne.

"This will happen Monday night. The Russians are bringing the weapons from the Ukraine as we speak. The shipment should be moving through Poland and arriving in Germany by tomorrow morning. You will be given the time and place the items will arrive tomorrow night."

"Good. What is the final destination? My people would like to know."

"Unfortunately, due to the need for secrecy, we will have to withhold that information until our people meet yours at the rendezvous point. We will have the manifest and the bill of lading along with GPS software on a flash drive prepared for your men. Rest assured, although your part of the operation is the most crucial, we expect it to be the most uncomplicated."

"We certainly hope so. Monsieur, if you would excuse me, I would take advantage of the facilities. I'll be right back."

"Tell your friends we expect this to be the first of many profitable transactions ahead," Chatillon said knowingly.

William was uncomfortable with the way this deal was set up, especially the gap between his end of the deal and Lucretia's. He knew she would be taking the handoff from the Germans. If she were to cause the deal to break down anywhere between the Alps and Italy, it would take a whole lo to keep her at the table. People such as these were just as likely to kill her as a precaution, regardless of how well INTERPOL set up her cover.

"Oh my gosh, William, is that you? I can't believe it!"

His blood froze as he turned to face Morgana Mc Laren and Fianna Hesher coming up to greet him. Morgana was dressed in an expensive purple dress, Fianna wearing a fashionable crimson dress that complemented each other perfectly. Morgana's Nicole Kidman looks had already caused numerous heads to turn as she moved through the steadily-growing crowd, many mistaking her for the glamorous actress. To make matters worse, she fell into his arms and gave him a long, loving kiss.

"Darling," he eased out of her embrace. "We've got to talk, all three of us. Let's go over to that table there."

"Why, what's wrong?" she asked as he took her by the hand and led the girls to a far corner.

"Fianna, Morgana, look," he said intently, "you know what I do for a living. Maybe not exactly, but you've got a good idea. Well, I'm in the middle of something right now. There are very dangerous men in this nightclub. If they saw me talking to you and I didn't mention it, they would be very suspicious."

"Couldn't you just…?"

"No. Never. Morgana, you're my fiancée."

"Wow," Fianna marveled. "Are they dangerous like Enrique Chupacabra?"

"He would fit in very well with these people, I can assure you. Morgana, please, I beg you. There's lots of other nice clubs around here. We'll make plans to meet somewhere out of town tomorrow or Sunday. I promise, darling."

"Well, okay,"

she said resignedly.

"You look absolutely gorgeous," he kissed her lips before giving Fianna a peck on the cheek. "Both of you. Don't do anything I wouldn't do."

"We won't," Fianna smiled merrily before following Morgana towards the exit.

William watched them leave before heading along towards the restroom. He knew this mission was about to take a very unexpected twist.

Two nights later, the man known as Jack Gain made a long-distance call before heading on his own date with destiny.

"Hello?"

"Darcy?"

There was a long pause.

"Why shouldn't I just hang up now?"

"For about a hundred thousand reasons."

"I got news for you, buddy, there's not all that many left."

"Why? Don't tell me you spent it all."

"No, but I got a new car, and found a little house for a good price. You told me I could use some of it, remember?"

"Is there at least 50K still left?"

"Of course," she was indignant. "I'm not a thief."

"All right, I'm gonna need it."

"Okay, I'll mail it to you. Let me get a pen."

"No, I'm gonna need you to bring it out. I can schedule you a flight."

"Oh, really? And where's this gonna be?"

"Toulouse, France."

"Okay, I know where that is."

"Like hell you do."

"Listen, buster, you think I didn't go to school? France is in Europe."

"I meant Toulouse, ye silly twit."

"So you call me after all this time to call me names?"

"Listen, doll. Something big's come up, really big. I'll need to keep you under wraps when ye get here because I'm working with some rough fellows. The payoff'll be worth it, though. We could end up with twice as much as last time, even more."

"You know, we've got enough now, we can have a good life. You don't have to keep doing whatever crazy shit you're doing."

"Are ye blootered, lass? A hundred grand's chickenfeed. Ye'd blow through that in two years."

"We could open our own business. Look, you know people. I saw you get decorated by the Queen of England. We're both young and healthy – well, maybe you not so much, but..."

"Don't get cheeky, Miss. Now see here. Ye'll withdraw the cash in hundred-dollar bills, and put it in a carry-on. For god's sake don't put any metal or stupid shite in the bag, just the money. Wrap it in a blanket or something."

"Why don't I just wire it to you?"

"These bastards I'm dealin' with are very well-connected. They may have some way to monitor large transactions. I can't take that chance. Besides, you and I haven't had any decent time together since last year, y'know."

"Oh, yeah? Pretty sure of yourself. Well, let me tell you something, you better not be fooling around with that Fianna bitch, you hear?"

"And what about that? I thought you two hit it off pretty well at Buckingham Palace."

"That's not the point. I don't share when it comes to guys. I'm serious. You screw around on me again and it's over, you hear?"

"Not to worry, love. I'm in thick with some evil bastards, and after I do 'em in, we'll be off on holiday to wherever ye like."

"What do you mean, do them in?"

"Just a figure of speech, love."

"Suppose they give you another medal? We'd have to stick around for that."

"Aye, I suppose so, but not for long?"

"Now listen, I'm serious. I'd better be the only woman there for you."

"Will you come off it? Now, here's the deal. I'll have a reservation for you at Miami International, it'll take you straight over here. You'll take a cab to Blagnac and ask for the Le Deauville Hotel. That's D-E-A-U-V-I-L-L-E. You just wait there and I'll call ye. If I don't call right away, ye can go out and fiddle about, but don't get caught up in anything. Got it?"

"You do the same, don't go getting all shot up again. How's your leg?"

"Right as rain. I'd forgotten all about it until ye brought it up."

"You know, I hate to admit it, but I really miss you."

"An' we'll make up for lost time. I'll see you real soon."

Jack took a flight to St. Gallen-Altenrhein Airport in Switzerland, where he was met by a Corsican at the exitway. He was escorted to the parking lot where a black van awaited, occupied by four other men. As the side door was opened for Jack, he was greeted by Jean-Paul Hornec.

"Glad you could make it."

"Aye, and I hope I'll be once this is over. Goin' from a drug deal to a cowboy job is quite a leap. I just hope it's not buyin' me time in a German prison."

"We've got this worked out and fine-tuned, I can assure you. This should not take us more than five to ten minutes."

"Eh, well, everything over five'll be in hot water, to be sure."

"Let me do the worrying, my friend."

They drove up the A14 North towards Bregenz in Austria just across the German border. They drove north through the Citytunnel toward the Bodensee lake, then veered right onto the Romerstrasse. Jack watched in fascination as the Frenchmen pulled a spiked chain across the road, setting a flashing emergency light atop the van and producing flashlights. They pulled the chain across, leaving only the fast lane open as they took up positions.

"So what's the deal, they don't have peelers out here?"

"We have good information on the target's travel time. Plus we put in a couple of false alarms to the local police department just in case."

"Amazin' there's no traffic," Jack peered up the deserted highway.

"There's no more flights coming in or out of the airport. Plus it's Monday. These fellows planned it very well."

"What fellows?"

"I see the van, I'm pretty sure it's their plates," one of the Frenchmen called over as he stared through high-powered binoculars up the road.

"All right, man your positions. Jack, you and I will walk up to the driver's side. I'll do the talking. Let's do it."

Jack fitted his silencer onto his Glock-17. He had not used it during the shootings in Ulster, hoping that the gunfire would attract the police and put an end to the foray. In this case, there was a bigger prize ahead if he could work this out. He watched as the van slowed to a halt as one of the gangsters waved the driver over with an incandescent wand.

"Yes sir?" the driver spoke German with an Italian accent.

"We are looking for an escaped convict," Hornec replied with his French accent. "We request that everyone step out of the vehicle and show you ID cards."

The driver and the man on the passenger side looked about furtively, assessing the situation. Jack anticipated their next move and jammed his pistol into the driver's ear, reaching in and switching off the motor before pocketing the key.

"Tell him to get the feck outta the van," Jack ordered Hornec. He did so as his men yanked the truck doors open, pulling the Italians out of the vehicle. It was a well-rehearsed operation, the Frenchmen pulling up their spiked chain and tossing it back into their van. They produced plastic ties and bound the Italians' wrists behind their backs, then marched them to Hornec's van. Three Frenchmen got in with them and drove the vehicle to the nearest exit. Jack, Hornec and a fourth gunman climbed into the Italians' van and followed the lead vehicle off the highway.

"It's here," the Frenchman told them. "They were using them as benches. One on each side."

Jack glanced back at the cloth-draped metal containers. He was familiar with them as they had been used to transport UDA[1] arms back in the day. Without their ammo clips, they could hold twelve short-stocked AK-47's each. It was enough to hold anything short of an armored convoy at bay. He remembered IRA[2] units taking on British

1. Ulster Defense Association
2. Irish Republican Army

convoys with those kind of arms, though with limited results. On the streets of NYC in the hands of suicide squads, the results would be devastating.

He watched as they turned in beneath the viaduct. They clambered out of the vehicle as the Frenchmen in the first van began hauling the Italians out onto the muddy concrete.

"So what's goin' on now?"

"Mission accomplished. If they get back up on the highway they'll get picked up by the police. If they stay down here long enough to cut free of the plastic, we'll be back in France by the time they do so."

"The driver's seen both our faces. So did the guy on the passenger side."

"Most likely they'll never see us again. Unless, of course, they want to risk their lives coming to France to find us."

"That's not good enough, Jean-Paul."

With that, Jack walked over to the Italians and forced them face down to the ground, one by one. Hornec and his men stared in apprehension as Jack stood over each Italian and shot them in the back of the head. As Jack's pistol jammed, the last Italian pleaded in German and Sicilian before one of the Frenchmen handed his gun to Jack. The gangster shrugged at Hornec as Jack finished off the last of the Italians. There was a dead silence before the Frenchmen began firing questions at Hornec in their native language. He answered them tersely before ordering them to load the two containers into their van. They pulled out their benches and replaced them in the Italians' van before climbing into their own vehicle.

"This was not in our plans, Jack," Hornec stared at him.

"Aye, well, ye had a fine plan except for the last part," Jack gazed into his eyes. "Maybe ye have the luxury of sittin' back in France until it all boils over. I don't."

"You'll have to come back with us to explain it."

"Well, you said I was gonna get to meet your honcho, so I guess this'll be a fine time. Quite a haul we're bringing back, eh?"

"Quite."

Jack and Hornec got into the van and they drove off, back onto the highway on the way to France by way of Switzerland. Jack would remain unaware that they were headed to the medieval city of Carcassonne for one of the most fateful encounters of his life.

Chapter Five

Once again the woman known as Lucinda Montesano was summoned to the mansion of Cesare Masseroli in Montelepre. She received a call before dawn informing her that the operation was postponed and her presence would be required at an emergency meeting. It was shortly after dark that evening by the time she arrived in her 2014 BMW. She was slightly nettled when the valets informed her that she would be unable to park her own vehicle.

"Those are the rules," the burly Sicilian explained. "For a meeting like this, we watch your car until you leave."

She was escorted to a different area of the mansion than she had seen the last time. An opened door led to a dimly-lit conference room where Cesare Masseroli sat at the head of a highly-polished table. At the opposite end sat Giovanni Cusimano along with three other middle-aged men. The last seat to Cusimano's left remained vacant for her.

"Thank you all for coming," Cesare opened the meeting. "I know you are all busy people, so we'll keep this as brief as possible. You are all aware that we were forced to postpone our transaction scheduled for this evening. Unfortunately there has been a tragic event that has forced this change of plans. The team of couriers transporting the goods across the German border was intercepted. The shipment was stolen and our soldiers were murdered."

The air was filled with sulphurous oaths and curses as his words impacted the men at table. Cesare raised a hand until the mutterings subsided.

"Who the hell could have done such a thing? Who even knew of this?"

"Lucinda, this is Don Anselmo from Naples. Seated to my right is Don Carlo from Bari, and to my left is Don Enrico from Calabria. Lucinda, as you all know, came highly recommended to us from the Pruszkow Mob in Poland. My friends, we do not know what was the cause of all this, but rest assured we will find out. The reason why I have called you all here is to resolve the problems this has created. The Russians are very concerned over this development and are threatening to cancel our arrangement. There is a team of mercenaries in Corsica who are bidding for the job, and the Russians are seriously considering their proposal."

"So what makes you think the Corsicans did not anticipate our move and set up the ambush?" Anselmo insisted. If they were tipped off by the Poles or the Germans, they could have easily arranged it. I told you there were too many parties involved with this thing."

"We've already discussed this," Cesare replied. "The Poles and the Germans are indispensable. This shipment is coming across the Ukraine through both countries. The Russians will not hear otherwise. We made the mistake of agreeing to send our people to Munich to bring the weapons to the Liechtenstein border. If we would have let the Germans bring the weapons, they would have borne the responsibility."

"I was expecting to take possession from a German team," Lucinda spoke up. "Why was I not informed?"

"We wanted to make sure you were going to be able to get the job done," Giovanni revealed. "The team captain was told to use his judgment before loading the cargo onto your truck. He is—was—one of our most trusted smugglers. He would have known within minutes whether you were capable of making the run. I got a good impression of you, but my colleagues insisted that we take precautions."

"Who is it that questions my ability?" she looked around the table.

"I've never done business with a woman before, let alone meet with one at a sitdown," Anselmo glowered.

"Neither have I," Carlo spoke up.

"So you question the justice of my colleagues in Poland who recommended me," she was nettled. "Why not set up a test? Name a city in Italy, and I will make a delivery there regardless of what obstacles you put in my way."

"We don't have time for this," Cesare insisted, staring at each of them. "If I may remind you, the Russians are merely giving us a taste of what is to come. They are testing our network to see if we are strong enough to carry what is to follow. If we cannot transport rifles, how are we going to be able to move the artillery they may be shipping next?"

"What artillery?" Enrico asked. "Do you know what kind of money we have invested in New York City? If those vampires get together with the ragheads and declare war on the streets, do you realize we stand to lose billions of dollars?"

"Remember your history, my friend, the history of this thing of ours," Giovanni said gently. "This can be a rebirth of our organization in America. Think of the Prohibition Era. When people are forced to depend on the black market for the things they want, the blackmarketer grows rich at the expense of the common business man."

"Do not forget, Don Giovanni, that Lucky Luciano cut a deal with the Government during World War II to guard the American harbors from saboteurs. That is why it took the FBI decades before they finally got to us. If we take sides with the Russians and the Government finds out, they will not rest until they wipe us off the map,"

Carlo was emphatic.

"Gilles Marotte in Corsica is arranging the transport across the Atlantic," Cesare reminded him. "There is no chance the Americans will ever trace the shipment back to us."

"Then why is Marotte not searching for those killers, those mercenaries?" Anselmo inquired.

"I have already sent word to him. As I said, justice will be done. What remains is how we will restore the confidence of the Russians in our network."

"That brings us back to Marotte," Anselmo retorted. "How do we know those mercenaries won't try it again? We need to take them out before we arrange another transport."

"Discussion will not change the situation," Giovanni said tersely. "Marotte is dealing with the possibility of starting a war with the mercenaries. There are rumors that they are part of an organization known as the Citadel. Very little is known about them. They are the dogs of war, they fight for money. It was after 9/11 when they began planning their own operations and working for themselves. The Corsican Mob has been playing cat-and-mouse with them until now. This is the first time they have shown aggression against a rival organization."

"I know some people with the Parisian Mob," Lucinda offered. "I can see whether they could be of service."

"There are already too many cooks in the kitchen," Anselmo waved a hand. "If anything, I say we cut the Corsicans out. Perhaps that will cause that Citadel to disappear as well."

"The Corsicans are the only thing that is keeping the Parisian Mob out of the deal," Cesare revealed. "Every Mob in Europe is hot for this deal. The Russians will spare no expense to retaliate if they are crossed by the Americans. The US and NATO can collapse their economy should they choose to do so. This terror threat is their ace in the hole, and they will bet everything they have on it. They have no other option."

"Here is the new plan," Giovanni declared. Everyone else realized that this had already been agreed upon between Cesare and Giovanni. "The Germans will bring the next shipment to the Liechtenstein border. Lucinda will be working with one of our soldiers in delivering the goods into Italy. We will transport the weapons to France, which will complete our part of the agreement."

"And who is this I'll be working with?" Lucinda asked.

"The individual is here waiting for this meeting to end," Cesare told her. "You will be introduced once out business is done here. Now, as far as the rest of you, I want you to ask favors from every connection you have outside of Italy, everywhere in Europe. The mission comes first, that is a priority. If one bullet is lost from the shipment, responsibility for the loss of the contract will be placed at the doorstep of your Family. Beyond that, my friends, I want to find every scumbag remotely connected with the Citadel."

"Gladly," Anselmo grinned wickedly as the others nodded in assent.

With that, they lowered their heads and joined in prayer. Lucinda soon realized they were invoking a Sicilian curse against their enemies and a blessing for their protection. She had heard these people were from a different century, but could not have imagined this.

"Come, my dear, let me introduce you to your new partner," Cesare led her down the corridor to the great hall where she had first met with him.

"Your people don't trust me, is that it?"

"Let me try to explain this to you. The reason why the Germans are not delivering it directly to the Corsicans in France is because they do not trust each other. This is the reason why we were brought in. The entire network has been designed to prevent any double-crosses or discovery by INTERPOL. No one expected this Citadel to move against us. The reason why you are here is to keep the Germans from trying to extend their connections into our territory. Our main concern is that no one tries to eliminate you."

Lucinda knew there was no point in arguing against such paranoia. She followed him into the hall and was surprised to see another woman sitting at the great table in the cavernous room.

"Lucinda Montesano, this is Concetta Pinzone. She will be accompanying you on your trip across Liechtenstein. I ask that you remain overnight as my guest so you can get to know each other better."

Concetta was a buxom brunette who had the jaded veneer of a Mafia princess. Lucretia did not want to deal with this but she knew Cesare would insist. She also knew that Concetta would be giving him a full rundown as soon as Lucretia hit the road.

"Well, let's get to bed," Lucretia yawned. "I'll have to leave to take care of business the first thing in the morning."

"Why, certainly," Cesare bade them goodnight. "There will be wine and cheese brought to your room. Have a wonderful evening."

Lucinda tried to avoid rolling her eyes. She knew this night was far from over.

It was an eight-hour drive from the Swiss airport to Toulouse, and Hornec was in an animated conversation on his cell phone the one time they stopped for gas. Jack appreciated the fact that these European gangsters were much like poker players, close to the vest until it came time to show their hand. Hornec said nothing until they finally arrived in downtown Toulouse. It came as no small source of relief to Jack, who might have expected the worst had he not been returned to town.

"All right, we need to switch vans and move the cargo," Hornec explained as they cruised to a halt in front of Jack's hotel. "We'll come back to pick you up at six. I'll give you a call before we head out."

"That'll be fine. See you then."

Jack went inside the lobby, then took the elevator up to his suite. He pulled off his clothes and turned on the shower before punching numbers on his cell phone.

"Hello?"

"Hey, love. Where are ye?"

"What, do you have amnesia?" Darcy Callahan demanded.

"Aw reet, don't start. Everything okay?"

"Well, I'm in bed. Are you coming over?"

"Aye, I just came t'my room for a change of clothes. I'll be there in a bit."

"Why didn't you come straight over here?"

"I just killed six fellows. I wouldn't feel right going' around in the same clothes, y'know."

"What? What did you just say?"

"It's a joke, ye twit. Now let me go, I'll be there in a bit. Order breakfast, I'm hungry."

"That's not funny. Why did you say six people? You wouldn't have given a number if it wasn't true."

"All right, a hundred and six. Happy? I'll be there inside the hour."

He jumped into the shower, hoping that the Austrian police had not found the bodies beneath the viaduct and plastered it all over the airwaves just yet. He was hoping to enjoy a reunion romp in the sack with Darcy before her interrogation commenced.

It was William Shanahan who woke up that morning and was astonished at what he saw on the BBC newscast. He immediately grabbed his cellphone and called Six at Vauxhall Cross.

"I'm watching the telly and don't believe what I'm seeing," William stood naked in front of the wide-screen plasma TV mounted on the living room wall. "This has Gawain written all over it. Did the girl know anything about this?"

"What are you referring to?"

"Listen, don't play games with me. Do you think I don't know about those other four people he killed near Newry? That's ten murders, and the operation's not a week old. Does Mark know about this? I thought this was Her Majesty's Secret Service. Have they turned this into an assassination bureau?"

"You know we don't discuss such matters on the phone. Disconnecting."

"I'm already on record for having objected prior to this…"

The line went dead.

Shanahan fought an impulse to smash the phone against the wall. It was happening all over again, Gawain being unleashed by MI6 to wreak havoc against enemies of the State. He nearly resigned after their last mission, and they appeased him by giving him the desk job he coveted for so long. Yet here they were entreating him to go back out on the field with the madman, and he was picking up right where he left off. He sat down on a chair facing the balcony overlooking the boulevard, unsure what to do next. Suddenly he had a flash of inspiration and called a US number.

"Hello."

"Hello yourself."

"Who the hell—? This sounds like William Shanahan."

"Very good. How've you been, fellow?"

"Just fine. What've you been up to?" Joe Bieber asked. He was Shanahan's CIA counterpart during the last mission, and they had gotten along well over the time they worked together. He was one of the few people in the business Shanahan considered a friend.

"Ah, you know, keeping busy. Say, I wanted to touch bases about that noise going on in the Ukraine."

"Classified. Are you on it."

"Yep."

"We've got something going with INTERPOL. Look, you know I can't talk."

"I know. Can I get on chat with you?"

"Yeah, sure. I'll go on now."

"Right."

Shanahan clicked off and went over to the suite's computer, logging on to the CIA's encrypted website.

-K

-Whuzup?

-Remember Gain?

-Sure.

-Loose cannon.

-No kidding.

-Need contact in Toulouse.

-Have him call.

He felt much better after he logged off. He took a shower and shaved before deciding to call Morgana. He needed a break from the action and she would be just what he needed. He had not heard from Gilles Marotte for a couple of days and figured the project was still pending.

It was only the news bulletin about the gangland killing in Bregenz that alerted him to what was happening. Not hearing from Marotte or Mark O'Shaughnessy was disconcerting. He felt like he was being kept out of the loop, and that was a very dangerous situation to be in.

"William! Where are you?"

"I'm at my hotel. I can meet you somewhere."

"Is Jack with you? Can I bring Fianna?"

"No, I'm here on special assignment. Sure, bring Fianna. She can play chaperone, keep us out of trouble."

"What kind of trouble were you thinking of?" she asked saucily.

"Now, darling, I told you I'm in a hard situation here. I just need to step away a bit and clear my head. I had you in my mind, so I figure we could have a drink. You'll just have to wait until I get back to London before we can get some quality time together."

"That's fine. I started thinking about it, and I shouldn't have just come out here without checking with you. I just thought that since you got that desk job, you wouldn't be working those undercover jobs."

"I wasn't expecting it. Look, I'll explain at a better time. Now, there's a little town not far from here called Blagnac. There's a place called La Vie en Rose on the Rue Dieudonne. I'll meet you there in an hour."

He proceeded to call Europcar at the airport and was somewhat nettled that all they had was a Nissan Maxima. He paid extra to have it driven to the hotel, and chose his tan leisure suit and a green shirt to wear along with his shoulder holster. He knew everyone had gone to ankle holsters, but he was old-fashioned in so many ways. He took comfort in the fact that Morgana liked him that way.

When he pulled up across the street from the restaurant, he was encouraged by the thought he had made the right choice. The girls were standing out front, dressed in light-colored silk dresses that complemented their beautiful legs. It was well-known that Fianna was as sexy as Morgana was beautiful, and between them they could break the heart of a statue. William waved to them and trotted across the street, exchanging hugs and kisses before they took his arms and headed inside. Most of the men in the area saw William as the luckiest man in Blagnac.

They spent an hour chatting as he explained to Fianna that he was doing some investigative work on an internal affair. It was not dangerous but he could not afford to be exposed lest the inquiry be compromised. Morgana knew better but allowed him to allay Fianna's apprehensions. She was also enjoying his display of tact and diplomacy in soothing her feelings over Jack not accompanying him. He explained that Jack was on a different assignment that was apart from his own assignment. Morgana delighted in seeing the diverse qualities of this man she had fallen in love with and planned to marry.

As they headed out to the front of the building once they finished a second drink, William insisted on paying their cab fare as he had errands to attend to. In reality he wanted to avoid driving around with them and possibly being spotted by the Corsicans. It would be far too easy for Chatillon to run a check on them and have the information in hand should he ever choose to leverage William for whatever reason.

"Hey, look over there!' Fianna pointed as a particularly voluptuous woman made her way down the street I their direction. She was wearing sunglasses and a tight-fitting summer dress, apparently not seeing the threesome at curbside. "Don't we know her?"

"Honey, is that Darcy?"

"Why, it may be."

"Darcy?" Fianna took a couple of tentative steps towards her.

"Oh my gosh! Fianna! And there's Morgana! And William! How are you doing?"

Darcy Callahan came over and exchanged hugs and kisses with the trio. More than ever, William Shanahan was the envy of the Rue Dieudonne.

"What are you doing here?" Fianna asked.

"Oh, I took advantage of a travel package. It starts and ends in Paris, they take you to these little towns and villages, you know. What are you doing here?"

"We had some time off and came to see Toulouse, the name's got such a pretty ring to it," Morgana replied sunnily. "It just so happened William was in town, so we all got together before he left."

"Gee, I wish I'd known. The tour's leaving in a couple of hours, otherwise I'd have planned to meet up with you."

"You haven't heard from Jack, have you?" Fianna wondered.

"No, not at all," she said with a regretful tone. "I thought for sure if you all got together, he'd be with you. I haven't seen him since that affair at Buckingham Palace last year."

"Well, ladies, I must be going," William said. "I believe that cab is available."

"Yeah, I gotta get back too," Darcy hugged and kissed everyone again. "Call me, you girls have my number, okay?"

"Sure. You still in Florida?"

"All year long. Give me a call, we'll get together."

William gave the cabbie a twenty before holding the door open for the girls.

"That bitch," Fianna grumbled. "What would a trailer trash chick like her be doing in France? She knows where Jack is."

"Well, she knows something I don't, in that case," William said, exchanging hugs and kisses with them as they entered the cab. "Darling, do give me a call if you happen across him."

"I sure will, even if I don't," she blew a kiss at him from the window. "Talk to you soon."

Darcy continued along the street, peering into the reflections of store windows to see if she was being followed. She looked about furtively before darting into Le Deauville, feeling like a James Bond girl with all the intrigue going on. She took the elevator up to her suite, where Jack Gawain awaited.

"Hey!" she called as she let herself into the room. "Guess who I just ran into!"

Jack was sitting in a hot bubble bath, greatly enjoying the respite after the ride back from Austria, wondering if he had bought himself a bullet in the head. Judging by the tone in her voice, he knew whatever this was, it wasn't good. He slowly slid down beneath the water, deciding he would drown himself if she didn't come in to question him soon.

Eventually she did, and he managed to deflect most of her questions before steering her into the bedroom for a sizzling lovemaking session. She was better than he remembered, and they exhausted each other a couple of times before falling into a deep sleep. They woke up late that afternoon, and he had room service bring up a steak and lobster dinner with champagne. She was quite satisfied when he finally dressed and took his leave to attend his meeting.

He spotted Chatillon's Citroen C4 Cactus parked by the curb near the hotel entrance, and slipped into the passenger seat as they headed for the highway. Chatillon sat behind him, two of the gunmen from the hijacking riding with them.

"We're about an hour away, depending on traffic. Did you get a good rest?"

"Aye, I sent out for a whore. She was pretty good, I think I'll have her back. D'ye have the guns in the trunk?"

"Surely you jest. We sent them back to the hideout as soon as we arrived."

"That's smart."

"Our organization rarely makes mistakes. When an error is made, we take careful steps to assure it never happens again."

The rest of the ride was punctuated only by small talk between the Frenchmen. He was wearing black cargo pants, in which he packed a .22 pistol as well as spare clips. It served as backup to the Glock-17 on his ankle. If he sensed that this was going to be a one-way ride, he would put one in the driver's head before shooting Chatillon behind him. He had seen situations like this before. Back in the day, when someone seriously botched an assignment, they would be called in for a UDA tribunal to assess the facts and decide whether negligence was a factor. Jack would stick by his story that he could not afford to have any of the Sicilian mobsters able to finger him in future. That was, in fact, his primary motivation.

When they reached the outskirts of Carcassonne, it was one of those classic moments in life. One could see magnificent pictures of the wonders of the world online, but looking at them with the naked eye was incomparable. The walled city was bathed in purple and golden light, its walls and turrets as if they had traveled back through the centuries. Jack savored the view until, at once, the car took a sharp right and headed down an obscure country road.

"Stopping for a piss break?" Jack asked nonchalantly, his fingers touching the pistol beneath his pants leg.

"You don't think we'd be operating inside the city, do you?" Chatillon allowed. "It would be pretty hard to escape if we were discovered, wouldn't you think?"

They traveled about a mile before the driver turned into a treeline that seemed impenetrable to the naked eye. Jack was about to draw his weapon before the Citroen bounced over three ridges and landed on a thirty-foot clearing facing a small waterfall.

"Do you have an itch, or were you planning to shoot somebody?" Chatillon chuckled.

"This looks like a perfect place for an ambush, if ye ask me."

"It would take an armored convoy to dislodge us from here, my friend."

To Jack's surprise, they drove directly into the waterfall, which was set up almost like a natural car wash in allowing access to the cave on the other side. The driver brought the car to a halt before the men bracketed Jack.

"At this point I'll have to check your weapons, *mon ami*," Chatillon was apologetic. "You are about to meet the leader of our organization. I'm sure you understand."

"Well, not much of a choice at this point, eh?" Jack smirked.

They patted him down and took his .22 but left him with his ammo clips. Chatillon led the way into the dark cavern, which was dimly illuminated with electric torches. The polished floor made the place resemble a nightclub.

They walked ahead about forty paces before stopping in front of what looked like an enormous red-and-black chessboard. The four men preceded him onto the floor, coming to attention and bowing their heads towards the dais against the far wall. Jack proceeded cautiously and suddenly came into full view. Upon the dais was a great throne, and seated upon it was a woman dressed in black ceremonial robed. She wore a tall veiled headpiece which hid her features completely.

"Jack Gain, this is the Black Queen of the Citadel," Chatillon introduced him.

He had no idea what to do in this surreal predicament. He decided his best bet was to bow slightly from the waist. She beckoned to them so that Jack and Chatillon stood at the edge of the dais, the two gunmen spread behind them.

"You are John Oliver Cromwell Gawain, formerly a brigadier with the Ulster Defense Association," she spoke through an electronic garbler. "You were sentenced to life in Maghaberry Prison but was reprieved by the British in exchange for your participation in a classified operation last year."

"Well, now that ye mention it," Jack allowed. If he made a mad dash he might reach the throne and catch her in a headlock, but they would probably gun him down before he made it.

"You turned the hijacking into a multiple murder without apparent need. Why?"

"Well, as I told yer men here, my own business requires occasional trips to the Continent. If we would've let those dagos off, they might've spotted me in future and did god knows what to find out where their weapons ended up. They were as much a threat to you as to me, milady."

There was a long pause which buoyed Jack's confidence.

"This unforeseen incident will have its repercussions. The Mafia will be searching far and wide for clues as to our identity. If we are discovered, it may prove costly. Yet it was our decision to bring you in with us. In exercising your judgment in creating this situation, your actions have affected all of us. It was as if you were one of us. We see no better option than to make you one of us."

"Why, that sounds grand," Jack managed a laugh. "Only I do have prior obligations."

"We all have prior obligations. This is a loose confederacy, so to speak. When we need you we will know where to find you."

"Well, then I guess I have no objections."

"There is one contingency. All of our brethren share the mark of the Citadel. It is placed beneath the shoulder muscle on the outside of your right arm. It should not be visible even if you roll up your sleeve. If it is seen, you can explain it as something you did after losing a drunken bet. It is no more noticeable than a poorly-healed injection mark."

"A tattoo, like? That may not be a good idea. It's the stupidest thing these young punks do these days. They have to send out to check yer prints, much less your blood or DNA. A tattoo, though—they got ye cold. I'm not the type, milady."

"Let me put it to you this way, Mr. Gawain. No one who enters here and does not belong to our brotherhood ever leaves this place alive."

"Well, since ye put it that way," Gawain exhaled tautly.

"Remove your shirt. It will be quick but painful. Consider it your initiation."

Gawain slowly pulled off his black leather jacket and his black pullover, then was startled by the sight of a small brazier being rolled in by four more gunmen.

"What th' shite? That doesn't look like a tat kit t'me."

"As you indicated, tattoos are for convicts and street thugs."

Jack cursed under his breath as he dropped his clothes to the dais and followed Chatillon over to the brazier. He turned sideways, facing the wall to the Black Queen's left as a gunman approached with the branding iron. The white-hot brand was barely a half-inch wide.

Gawain hissed as the metal burned into his flesh. He tried to brace himself but was nowhere nearly prepared for it. Somehow he had the willpower to keep from bolting away from the indescribable pain. He realized that Chatillon was holding his shoulders once the metal was taken away, and all he could think of was killing someone for a piece of ice. He thought of what cattle had to endure, only they had an inch-thick hide. Jack cupped the throbbing wound until one of the men squeezed a sponge of cold water over it. He reached for the sponge but the gunman pulled it away.

"Wait a couple of minutes so you do not further harm the skin," Chatillon came from behind him. "You did well, my friend."

As the Black Queen beckoned them, Jack went to put his clothes back on after being given a bandage and a piece of dressing by one of the men.

"You are one of our brotherhood, you belong to the Citadel," the Black Queen revealed. "We will always know where to find you. Whenever you need a favor from us, you will contact Chatillon. He is your godfather and sponsor. He will speak for you until the day of the death of either of you."

"So, is this like a perk deal, like discounts on hotels and rentals?" Jack remained cocky.

"Something like that," they could discern mirth in the Black Queen's tone. "If you let us know you are in Europe, we can make your stay a bit more pleasant and profitable."

With that, the men lined up before the dais and bowed their heads. The Black Queen raised her hand in acknowledgement before they took their leave.

"You lousy bastard," Jack snarled at Chatillon after he was handed his guns back. "Ye knew this was gonna happen."

"Would you have come if I told you?" Chatillon smiled curtly. "Few men handle the pain as well as you did. The Black Queen will not forget that."

"So what's up with that?" Jack asked as they turned around in the circular passageway and headed back through the waterfall. "You've got a woman running things? What's that about?"

"Her grandfather was with the French Foreign Legion, as are most of our senior officers. He was killed at Dien Bien Phu in Viet Nam. The Citadel was his creation, a brotherhood of legionnaires who joined as a mercenary force after France abandoned the war. His son was personally trained by the mercenaries. He rose to command after numerous operations in North Africa and Southeast Asia during the Sixties. He, in turn, trained his daughter. She rose through the ranks during the Serbian War in the Nineties. Attrition is an enzymatic factor in this life of ours. When he was killed in action, his wishes were honored in making her our leader."

"Well, I'll take yer word for it. We going back t'Toulouse?"

"No, you are our guest of honor. We will take you for dinner and some nightlife, and put you up in a four-star hotel. We'll have you driven back tomorrow any time you like."

"Well, I don't know if I'm up for it. This thing hurts like a bitch."

"Here is some hydrocodone," Chatillon handed a bottle over Jack's shoulder. "Take one at intervals, give them some time to kick in. They are very powerful."

"All right. I just hope there's some decent women wherever we're going."

"You can chase after whatever you like, or we can have some sent in, as you wish."

The men laughed along with Jack, who suddenly thought of Darcy.

Not only was he going to have to listen to her shit tomorrow, but he would have a time explaining his new brand.

It was what he would consider a classic example of adding insult to injury.

Chapter Six

William Shanahan turned onto the Rue Roschach and cruised into L'Union, a suburb not far from Toulouse. He parked near the Campanile Toulouse Nord L'Union hotel and restaurant, which appeared as a cafeteria of sorts. He strolled into the restaurant, looked around and saw a familiar figure waving at him. He was glad to recognize Joe Bieber from the CIA in the far corner. They shook hands and clapped each other's shoulders before taking seats at the table.

"This is a surprise," William smiled. "I thought for sure you were sending a flunkie."

"It was too much of a temptation," Joe grinned. "Besides, there's a INTERPOL meeting right around the same time as the NATO conference next week. I didn't see the harm of coming in early and catching up with an old friend. You look good. How the heck did they talk you into going back out on the field? I thought you'd realized your dream by getting that desk job. And, by the way, congratulations on getting that medal from the Queen. We heard about it back at the office. I was damn proud of you."

"Thanks. Well, it was a case of Mark pleading and nagging. He mentioned the Prime Minister had asked about the fellows who aborted Operation Blackout, and that was the kicker. When they start playing the Queen and Country card, it's pretty hard to resist. Bottom line, they needed someone to keep track of Jack Gawain and to make sure our INTERPOL contact wasn't killed. Considering the fact I haven't heard anything from either of them since we were deployed, I can only guess everything's still fine out there. How's things on your end?"

"After that Snowden affair, lots of people in the spy community are worried about how many more leaks we have in our bucket," Joe admitted. "We're not sharing as much with MI6 as before, and vice versa. Plus, with this thing looking more and more like a potential military confrontation, everybody's playing it close to the vest."

"The bottom line is that our cousins at Langley will always be our cousins," William replied after thanking a roving waitress for coffee. "And, of course, there'll always be wayward sorts such as us who don't have a problem disregarding the restrictions."

"Right now NATO's very concerned about the use of Spetznaz[1] units throughout Europe. You've seen how dangerous it was in Northern Ireland. The Poles and the Germans have enough trouble with the Russian Mob. If the Spetznaz starts working with the Mob, we're gonna be seeing major problems."

"Actually that's what we're looking at. We're trying to analyze their logistics along Southern Europe. We're hoping if we can hit these gangsters hard they'll start having second thoughts. Dealing narcotics isn't quite the same as selling guns to terrorists."

"Yep, you can't get the death penalty or get sent to Guantanamo for selling drugs. Of course, if the socialists have their way and close Gitmo, we're not going to have it to scare the bad guys with."

"That's odd. In the UK, they treasure human rights but don't care whether London is covered with security cameras. In the US, your privacy is sacred but Guantanamo's okay for now."

"The problem is what's happening on the Russian side," Joe slowly stirred sweetener into his coffee. "There's a place called Dagestan we call Terrorist University. People have no rights there. The Spetznaz snatch people off the streets in broad daylight, and they're never seen again. Kids either wait their turn, or go into the Forest. When they come out of the Forest, they're born again killers."

1. Russian Special Forces

"One of those Tsarnaev brothers, he was over there before the Boston Marathon bombing, wasn't he?"

"Exactly. Only there's two sides to that coin. The Spetznaz troops have their homes bombed, their headquarters blown up. Their comrades die in their arms in the street. We're worried that some of those troops are given the option of working undercover in Eastern Europe after a tour in Dagestan."

"Dammit, that sounds grim."

"That's not the worst of it. We're hearing reports of a place called the Citadel somewhere in France that is modeling itself after the Forest."

"Really?" William's gut clenched, yet he displayed no emotion. "What's that about?"

"It sounds so outlandish that the jury's out as to whether it's some underworld legend or not. They say there's a female mercenary out there they call the Black Queen. She went to Dagestan to study their methods. She has a small army that has been hiring out in ops across Africa and Eastern Europe since the Nineties. If the Russians manage to hook up with them, it could be bad news. Provided there is such a place."

"I'll be sure and have them pass it along to Jack. Say, perhaps you could do me a favor?"

"Sure."

"They've got us working with a female INTERPOL agent, and I don't know very much about her. MI6 has it set up that way, but maybe you could give me some background."

"I can do that. Write the name down for me."

"It's Lucretia Carcosa," William jotted it down on a napkin. "Supposedly she's been running undercover operations out of Poland. I just want to know what kind of experience she really has. She told us a story about taking a bullet on the field. Frankly, she looks like a model or an actress. I don't know what I could expect if I had her watching my back."

"Hopefully it won't come to that. You just stay in the rear with the high-tech gear, my friend. I haven't had a gun pointed at me since I joined the Company, and I don't ever intend to."

"Well, you know Jack. I just have this sinking feeling that I'll be pulling that bastard's arse out of a major firefight before this is over."

"Just make sure you bring the Cavalry with you when you go."

"Or else I'll call you," William grinned.

Nearly six hundred miles away, the man called Jack Gain sat at a table with Danny Di Benedetto. The captain of Don Anselmo's crew had come out with his top lieutenant and six gunmen for this sitdown at Hostaria Dino E Toni, which was located a short distance from the Vatican Museums. Once again the Mob seating arrangements were evident to those in the know who avoided the corner table on the patio. Di Benedetto and his lieutenant sat glowering at the man in black across from them. They were bracketed on each side by pairs of gunmen at the adjoining tables. They sipped wine and sampled the *antipasti della casa* though listening intently to every word spoken at the meeting table.

"So you and your crew want to sell us back the weapons that were stolen from us in Bregenz," Di Benedetto took a bite of *bruschetta*. "For twice what it's worth. Let me ask you something. What makes you people think we would even consider paying that?"

"The Russians," Jack took a sip of cappuccino. "I'm pretty sure ye haven't told the Russians yer people lost their shipment. Right now yer scramblin' t'put together a similar package an' hope it passes, but ye don't know what they had in the containers. If there were any special items that don't show up at the final destination, they'll know ye tampered with their goods. I don't think they'll like that one bit."

"Lemme ask you something," the lieutenant glowered. "What makes you think I don't pull a cowboy here and shoot you right in the fuggin' face right here at this table?"

"Two reasons," Jack smiled. "See the black van parked by the curb near the entrance? And ye see the one that's just pullin' up alongside us?"

"Yeah?" the lieutenant and his men stared at both vehicles.

"Now watch this. I raise my right hand..." they saw the vehicle by the entrance's emergency lights flash. "And I raise my left hand."

The emergency lights of the van by the curb closest to them blinked.

"There, ye see. Both vans are filled with explosives, enough to take out half a city block. I could give ye a head start and ye wouldn't have time t'get away. Not t'mention all the priests and Vatican workers and assorted holy men cavortin' around here. It'd send ye t'hell with a whole lot more bad karma than yer already carryin' with ye."

"Listen, you sick fuck," Di Benedetto lost his cool. "Who do you represent? What are you people trying to prove?"

"Well, it's complicated," Jack said casually. "We're a small but powerful operation. We think we can help the Russians get their mission accomplished but right now there's too many cooks in the kitchen, as they say. We're figurin' if we leverage you out, it'll make it a lot easier to get this thing done."

"Okay, look," Di Benedetto held a hand up to his lieutenant, who was about to explode. "Let's back up and look at this thing rationally, like good businessmen. Put yourself in my place. I'm sitting across a table from some crazy son of a bitch who says he's got two truckloads of dynamite sitting at the curb. Okay, fine. But he's trying to sell me a hijacked shipment he stole from me for twice its value. Plus he wants me to back out of a multimillion dollar arms deal. Now, obviously I'm not the man at the top of the mountain. I got to answer. Now what do I go back and tell the man on the mountain when he asks me who's making this shithouse crazy offer?"

"Got a pen?"

One of the men at the nearby table passed a felt-tip pen to Di Benedetto, who pushed it over to Jack. Gawain casually sketched a small marking on a napkin resembling the one that had been branded onto his arm.

"There. Does that mean anything to you?"

"What the fuck is that?" the lieutenant growled.

"Hold on," Di Benedetto raised his hand again. "So this is you."

"Aye. Y'see, this whole thing has gotten very complicated. Y'got the Yanks and the Brits, NATO, INTERPOL, and god knows who else stickin' their noses in the so-called kitchen, where we already know there's far too many cooks. Using that analogy, the Russians have paid for the meal in advance and are wonderin' what's holdin' it up. When they don't get what they paid for, they're not goin' t'be lookin' for their money back. They'll be lookin' for a different kind o' payback, and lotsa people are gonna get killed."

"Okay, help me through this," Di Benedetto stared at him. "I buy the weapons back. I complete my end of the deal. Then I just walk away, and you and your people take over."

"Well, if that's how yer lookin' at it. The way I see it, yer payin' for a valuable lesson in how not t'transport stolen weapons. When ye get it to your counterparts for delivery across the Atlantic, yer even with the Russians and ye just walk away. That narrows it down to the Corsicans, and I'm quite sure they're goin' t'walk away as well. They're in no better position than you. That leaves us and the Russians. And NATO, INTERPOL, the UK, the USA and all these other feckin' monsters out there. Y'see, this isn't about th' guns we're sellin' back to ye. This is just an appetizer, a taste. They're gonna send the real deal along as time goes by. Maybe a chemical weapon, maybe a mini-nuke, who can say. Yer not gonna know when or where any more than ye know what was in those containers we lifted off ye. An' then yer fecked. They declare the Sicilian Mob, the American Mafia, yer mothers and fathers, aunts and uncles, as terrorists. An' that's somethin' ye want no part of. That's what I'm takin' off yer plate today."

Di Benedetto narrowed his eyes, allowed a small smile to cross his lips, then leaned back in his chair.

"That's a good story. Who made it up, them? The Citadel?"

"Nay, I had a bit o' input meself, y'know."

"Let me tell you something. The Corsican Mob is a pimple on my dick. They're a glorified crew as far as we're concerned. When we whistle, they sit up and beg. You ain't narrowing this deal down to shit. We're getting paid to bring those shipments from Point A to Point B. We don't give a shit if they put it on the White House lawn after that. All this end-of-the-world bullshit of yours don't mean jack to me. Here's my counteroffer. You give me back my containers and I'll forget this whole thing ever happened. I'll do my best to convince my boss that the six guys who got whacked in Bregenz was just part of the deal going sideways."

Di Benedetto reached over and picked up the napkin before Jack, then produced a lighter.

"Ever see this in the movies?"

He lit the napkin and burned the tiny citadel etching before quickly snuffing it out.

"See, this is the real world. This is the way things work. You ever hear that saying, when in Rome? Well, you're sitting in it. Welcome to Rome. You go back and tell this Citadel of yours that we're not going nowhere. The Paris Mob, the Corsican Mob, all these Mickey Mouse gangs the Russians got building the pipeline, they don't mean shit. Right now, you got my containers and six dead soldiers to account for. That's the reality here."

"Okay, I suppose we'll just have t'go about doin' things the hard way from here in," Jack exhaled. "I was just tryin' t'be helpful."

"Where the fuck you going?" Di Benedetto demanded as Jack stood up.

"I just had th' coffee. Ye can cover that, can't ye?"

Jack motioned with his right hand, and the Mafiosi hunkered down as the door to the van near the entrance of the restaurant flew open. At once a ramp slid out and a bunch of senior citizens appeared, waiting to emerge for their scheduled brunch. They watched as Jack slung his leg over the railway surrounding the patio. He sauntered toward the van parked at the curb, and the door flew open so he could join the three men seated inside.

"Sally, get the car!" Di Benedetto fumed. "We follow those guys! I'm gonna settle this thing right now!"

"Yo, Di B," the lieutenant reasoned. "We hit them here downtown, Don Anselmo's gonna have our asses."

"I don't give a shit, I'll answer for it."

One of the soldiers jumped the rail and raced for their SUV parked at the end of the street. He hopped inside and gunned the engine, sailing to a halt at the curb where his teammates were vaulting the rail. They clambered inside and the truck bolted away, nearly hitting a taxicab as they set out in pursuit of the black van. They peered into the second van as they passed, but the driver was nowhere in sight.

As they whipped around the corner, they spotted the vehicle sitting on the corner two blocks away. The gunmen began pulling their weapons, coming to a screeching halt alongside the van. Its doors were wide open and its emergency lights blinking, but it had been abandoned with no one but pedestrians in sight.

It was the next evening when Concetta Pinzone arrived at the rendezvous point on the outskirts of southern Salzburg. She arrived at the airport earlier and found the car where it was supposed to be parked near the Lufthansa office. About a half hour later, she spotted the Continental Curios van parked on the side road and spotted the female driver behind the wheel reading a road atlas. She drove down the street, pulled up behind it and backed up so that they were parked back-to-back. Concetta got out and walked over to the passenger side, climbing in alongside the driver.

"Find what you're looking for?"

"Ready to go," the woman spoke English with a French accent, gunning the engine.

Concetta was an anomaly in the Sicilian Mob. Though she could never become a made member because of her gender, she was an associate in excellent standing. She was an assassin who had pulled over thirty hits in her career. She was a voluptuous woman, about five pounds overweight, with thick flowing chestnut hair and sexy Italian features. She was in her thirties and looked very much like a pampered matron in her $200 dress suit. Only she and the woman called Lucinda Montesano would change into blue jumpsuits and combat boots before they reached their destination.

She didn't think much of Lucinda though she didn't have much to go on. As a rule, she knew that female operatives were of limited value in combat situations. Their female instincts often led to a fatal error. They looked before they leapt, and that split second could mean the difference between life and death. This deal was supposed to be a straight delivery job, and if this bitch screwed up Concetta would put a slug in her head and tell the Don she had an accident.

They spent the night together at Don Cesare's mansion a couple of evenings ago. Lucinda was nice enough, a typical Frenchwoman with her girly-girl perspectives on life and traveling around Europe. Concetta could hold a conversation as well as the next person, and they prattled on about restaurants and shopping until they finished the bottle of *chianti* the Don had sent to their room. They were next scheduled to meet here, and Concetta just wanted to finish up and head back to Palermo to relax until a real assignment came along. Fifty grand for a hit was a worthy score to deposit in her Swiss bank account. Five grand for a job like this was a weekend on the Riviera.

This run should have been a piece of cake. Austria was considered neutral territory. The police here just did their job, no more or less. As long as dealers were merely passing through and not setting up shop, it was laissez faire in most cases. The Federal Police were tipped off occasionally by the German authorities when there were some big loads moving through. This was probably not going to fit the bill.

They set out on the B150 en route to Pauernfeind and saw the lead vehicles on the side of the road as if one had stopped to help the other. Lucinda hit the emergency lights and pulled up behind the second vehicle as the lead van rolled back onto the highway. The second vehicle paused before following the van, and Lucinda gave them two car lengths before moving on. The women saw the vehicles take the next exit and continue along the east road into the countryside. It was almost dark and there was light traffic as people were on their way home from work.

She saw them pulling into a farm property surrounded by a metal barricade resembling those along the highway. She was mildly surprised and assumed that the land was used to store farm machinery. The cost of such a barricade would not have been justified by the transport of livestock. Yet she did not see any treadmarks on the gravel pathway or the roadside. Her main concern was if these *mamalukes* were being monitored, there would be no way to drive through the barricades without wrecking their vehicle. She never liked being in a tight squeeze where there was no secondary point of egress, but she was not the one who put this thing together.

"Listen, you stay here by the gate until they signal us," Concetta warned Lucinda. "I don't like the setup here."

They watched as two men emerged from the barn next to the small farmhouse where three SUVs were parked. The men opened the front gate, a heavy steel barrier set on metal hinges affixed to the surrounding barricade. The vehicles ahead of them rolled directly toward the barn door, which was being opened from within. The gate guards began waving at Lucinda, who dutifully drove through.

"Don't go all the way inside," Concetta insisted. "Tell them we will wait here."

"They are going to have to load the containers onto the truck," Lucinda insisted, her cap pulled down over her eyes so her features were obscured. Just as they had planned, they would appear as young men from a distance. Once they got back on the road and changed clothes, no one would suspect two women driving a curio delivery truck of anything unusual.

"They sent me along to guarantee security," Concetta snapped at her. "I don't like the looks of this. Do as I say."

"You are here to make sure I don't get waylaid again. I am the one in charge of the transport. They are not going to carry the containers all the way over here. Don't be foolish."

"I don't want that gate closed behind us!" Concetta admonished her.

Just as she expected, the men at the gate pulled the barrier closed behind them. Concetta watched in apprehension as a deathly calm fell over the property. At once hell broke loose as the sound of automatic fire echoed throughout the barn. They watched the gunmen from the truck in front of them spilling out of both sides of the vehicle, jacking clips into their Uzis.

"What did I tell you, fool!" Concetta yelled, pulling her Glock from her ankle holster. She rolled down her window and began firing at the gate guards, taking them both out with head shots despite her poor firing position. "Go into reverse and smash through the gate!"

Lucinda shifted gears and the van hurtled backward. It crashed with great force against the gate, nearly ripping it off its hinges. Yet the vehicle groaned to a halt, the 'check engine' light flashing on the dashboard as the chassis buckled under the impact. Both women rolled out of the van on the driver's side and ducked for cover as automatic fire shattered the windshield. Concetta flattened herself against the vehicle and grabbed Lucinda by the sleeve of her jumpsuit.

"All right, we'll make a run for the gate," she instructed Lucinda as the smell of gasoline from the ruptured tank permeated the air. "You roll yourself over, right side first, and stay on the ground when you land in case they start firing at us."

"What about the others?" Lucinda protested. "Aren't you going to try and help them escape?"

"I am not responsible for them. I am responsible for you. Now move it!"

The women made a break for the gate. Suddenly Concetta felt a heavy impact on her upper back near her shoulder. She instinctively reached back and could feel something sticking out from her back. She was relieved at the sight of Lucinda doing as she was told, rolling over the metal bar and remaining where she fell. Concetta fired a couple of shots behind her to cover her move, then did a barrel roll over the gate. Only it felt as if a parachute had broken her fall, and she clumsily toppled face first onto the ground before everything went black.

"This is disappointing news. My colleagues were anticipating the first shipment as a beta run. We were expecting this to be the first of many profitable deliveries."

"As were we, my friend. Unfortunately we cannot account for the reliability of others who are involved with this enterprise. I have been assured by the Russians that they are doing everything in their power to resolve this issue and complete the first transaction. They say that they are combining the items into one large shipment that will be worth nearly a quarter million dollars. If we are able to get these to the US in a timely manner, the next delivery will be significantly larger and far more profitable."

William had been summoned to Propriano once again to meet with Gilles Marotte. He was told of the delay caused by the Sicilian Mob and was certain it was due to Jack and Lucretia's success. Yet he had not gotten any updates from MI6 and had to put on an air of displeasure when confronted by the news. Obviously it was causing the Russians to adjust their schedule, but things might be moving along faster than their NATO counterparts could afford.

"What kind of ordnance would we be transporting? It certainly would make a difference of they were planning to move RPG-7's. We could well afford the kind of lawyers who could keep our operatives out of Guantanamo if they were caught moving AK-47's. RPG's, though – that could get our people buried alive if the proper precautions weren't taken."

They sat on a garden terrace overlooking the countryside, and a waiter brought them a bottle of chianti with a loaf of bread and cheese. Marotte sipped his wine and sat back, enjoying the breeze on this idyllic day.

"Do you play chess, William?"

"Occasionally."

"As do I. I don't have the time or the patience to improve my game, and I don't like losing, so why bother. They say the Russians are the best chess players. Their winters are the worst on the planet, so their earliest memories are of being stuck playing indoors. By the time they begin school, they've played thousands of games. Their teachers are able to connect with them using chess in analogies about life. They are taught to be very careful, to take precautions rather than move ahead recklessly and suffer loss. This is the way we Corsicans think, we respect that."

"It's a smart way of thinking."

"The Russians move their pawns first. They exercise caution. If the pawns are taken, they try something else. When they see an opportunity, they strike quickly and ruthlessly. They played a gambit with the Sicilians, and it failed. They are going to strike hard with the *Unione* and the Council. We must not fail, my friend."

"So what am I to tell my associates? That the Russians are going to be taking a great risk with this next shipment?"

"Not so much this one as the next one. This one, however, will test the mettle of both our organizations. If we fail as the Sicilians fail, not only will we be cut out of the network, but there may be reprisals. These people are playing for keeps."

"Reprisals? Do they have intentions of punishing the Sicilians?"

"From what I understand, they are very unhappy about how the Sicilians have handled their end of the bargain. It reflects badly on the rest of us. The Russians feel such negligence should not go unpunished. I do believe the penalty is warranted."

Concetta Pinzone woke up with blurred vision. She shook her head and realized she was tied to a chair at a metal table. She was stripped to her underwear, and the metal chair and table were cold against her skin. Her ankles were tied to the front legs and her wrists to the supports of the backrest. Her breasts rested upon the tabletop, and the chair seemed to be anchored down. She looked to her left and saw Lucinda tied up in like manner. She looked across the table and saw Vito, one of the gunmen assigned to the transport. He was chained naked to a punching bag support. His elbows were bound behind his head so that his lower arms dangled helplessly in the air. He too was positioned so that his genitals laid upon the table.

"I am Rudenko," a man in camouflage fatigues walked casually from the shadows in the cinder block room to the head of the table. "I am the person in charge of this operation for which you were contracted. We have a saying in Russia. The first time, the embarrassment is yours. The second time, the embarrassment is mine."

He spoke Italian with a thick Russian accent, walking over to Vito as if they were the only ones in the room. Vito began pleading and begging to no avail.

"We pardoned you the first time when your team was hijacked in Bregenz. We were led to believe it was a well-planned attack. This time, however, you made a stupid mistake. First you send these two whores as your rear guard. You actually trusted them to bring our weapons through Switzerland. They couldn't even get you out of an ambush."

"We had no idea what was happening," Vito pleaded, his hands turning blue from the lack of circulation. "We did exactly as we were told. We drove through the gate into the barn building. We had no idea the Germans had been intercepted. How could we possibly know they had been compromised just as our people were in Bregenz?"

"We told you that INTERPOL and NATO were all over this deal," Rudenko snarled. He stood 6'4", 300 pounds of solid muscle, with a Viking-like beard and flowing hair beneath his black beret. "We told you that if just one of our deliveries were intercepted, it would give the American President an excuse to deploy troops to Eastern Europe to set up a blockade. It was fortunate for us that one of your competitors chose to expose your weakness in taking your business from you. Not so fortunate for you."

He melted into the shadows, then reappeared with a stainless steel mallet encased in rubber. He tapped the mallet against his palm as he walked up to Vito.

"I was stationed in Cuba for a short time a few years ago," he explained. "I was repelled and fascinated with the peasants' way of bringing a new bull onto their pasture. They would use the old bull as a plow animal. The way they would do this is by crushing his testicles.

Of course, there was a fifty-fifty chance the animal would survive the torture. I always felt sorry for the bulls. Yet I can never find it in myself to feel sorry for a man who compromises the trust of his business partners."

Concetta watched in horror as Lucinda lowered her head, squeezing her eyes shut. Vito began howling in terror, but was unable to move as Rudenko began measuring his shot. At once Vito's voice reached ever greater decibels before gurgling to a deathly moan as the hammer rose and fell. Concetta counted ten blows, half of which were far more than Vito could bear. Rudenko grabbed his hair and raised his face, showing the unconscious man's eyes rolled back in his head. Blood ran down his jaws as he had cracked almost every tooth in his mouth.

"And now we will see if you two whores will be able handle it as well, after I reduce your cow udders to pancakes."

Concetta began to plead for her life, but before she completed a sentence she felt a sharp pain in her left tricep. She glanced over at Lucinda, who had a uniformed man standing at her side. At once she felt a dizzying sensation before slipping into unconsciousness once more.

Chapter Seven

William Shanahan had read about the rumors of a Russian backlash against the impending NATO sanctions. He rose before dawn and got the latest news on the Internet. There was also an encrypted message from Six indicating that he needed to be at the airport by 10 AM. He had taken the last flight from Palermo and was not looking forward to another trip this early. He did not like the way this assignment was going down, and intended to let his opinion be heard.

He jumped into the shower, nettled by the thought of Gawain and Lucretia operating on their own without giving him any feedback. The killing of Emiliano Murra last year remained as a sword of Damocles over his head. If somehow they obtained any information as to his complicity, he was a dead man at best. He knew the Corsicans were as bloodthirsty as the Sicilians, and they were just as inclined to send grisly messages to their enemies. If either one of them blew their cover, William would never know until it was too late. Someone had to open up this pipeline or he was going to go right over Mark's head for better access.

The cell phone went off just as he began dressing, and he saw the text message indicating another encrypted message was on the way. He got on the Internet and saw it was from Joe Bieber. He then accessed the CIA database and saw that Joe had information of Lucretia. It was a welcome bit of info that he would follow up on once he got his next task at the airport. He needed to know what Lucretia was all about. He had everything he needed to know about Gawain.

He decided to take a cab to the airport. He left the rental car at the garage, comfortable in knowing that he had a hand-held sweeper in the trunk with which he could check the car for tracking devices. The car would become an enticing target for anyone wanting to trace his movements. He would also spread invisible powder along the entry points in his room, and instruct the front desk that his room was not to be disturbed. He would turn this rendezvous into an opportunity to ensure he was not being monitored.

As soon as he arrived, he got a call on his cell phone to report to the security office. He headed over and was met by two plain-clothes officers who escorted him to a private plane at the further-most end of the grounds. He boarded the British Aerospace 125 and was informed he would be flying to Lake Geneva for a meeting with Mark O'Shaughnessy. It made sense as the headlines indicated a NATO meeting was scheduled there in the next couple of days. British security would already be in place to prevent anyone from following the operatives into town.

Upon arrival, he was driven to a chalet along the outskirts of town. There had been a light snow that dusted the landscape just enough to give it a greeting card look. He was let out at the gate surrounding the property where two plainclothes agents announced his arrival via radio. He was given a ride on a golf cart to the main entrance where two more agents permitted him access. Yet another agent accompanied him to the rear hall of the spacious mansion where the meeting was being held.

"Well, well, look who's here."

Shanahan was surprised to see Jack Gawain on one side of the massive oak table, facing a haggard-looking Lucretia Carcosa across from him. At the head of the table was Mark O'Shaughnessy, dapper in a black $1,000 Savile Row suit. He was flipping through dossiers and barely nodded as the agents closed the heavy wooden doors from outside.

"I imagine they've kept you two rather busy," Shanahan took a seat at the far end of the table. Mark responded by closing a file and pulling his electronic tablet before him.

"I thought I'd take advantage of this lull in the action by calling this meeting and comparing notes. I'm sure everyone has questions concerning all the rumors surfacing in the media as of late."

"Aye, I've got some questions, for sure," Gawain blustered. "How deep do I have to go t'get t'the bottom of this thing? I've seen neither hide nor hair of these two, and I'm in so far that I can't see the light behind me. These Corsicans are cold-blooded killers, I'll tell ye. If they suspect me of being crooked, they'll smoke me as soon as look at me. I've enough now t'take 'em down, let's do 'em in and get it over with."

"I don't know what he's on about, but I'm up to my neck in Corsicans as well," Shanahan admitted. "I've been out to Palermo twice, and it's the lion's den as far as I'm concerned. I agree with Jack, this is right about on the level with infiltrating an Al Qaeda cell in Iraq. I'm just waiting for someone to come in with a message to waste me on the spot."

"I've had enough, I'm out," Lucretia's lovely blue eyes were darkened from lack of sleep. "I am requesting that my superiors pull me off this case. I can't describe what I've seen so far. I could've been killed, I'm not sure why I'm still alive. There are Russian Special Forces in southern Europe, this needs to be escalated immediately."

"Russians?" Gawain's eyes lit up. "Now we're gettin' somewhere."

"How'd you know they were Special Forces?" Shanahan wondered.

"He identified himself before he crushed a man's testicles with a hammer before my eyes!" she vented. "These underworld gangs are double-crossing each other and the Russians have taken it upon themselves to expedite the shipments. These gangsters are no match for these commandos. I am not going to sacrifice myself as a pretext for NATO to confront this open threat!"

"Talk about busting balls," Gawain managed a chuckle.

"I beg your pardon!" she was indignant.

"Everyone settle down," Mark grew impatient. "This is the reason why I called this meeting. We all needed to get some feedback from one another."

"If I may, sir," Shanahan asked, "what input were you about to offer us?"

"Well, since you asked. NATO is well aware of rumors of Russian operatives making connections in Western Europe. This is the reason why we created this task force. You may be aware by now that the initial shipments were intended to test the waters, to gauge the resiliency of their network. We are aware that they are dealing exclusively with the Corsicans at this juncture. Their Federal Security Service has bought into our European Council scheme and is convinced that it will be able to transport their ordnance across the Atlantic. Or at least that's what the CIA and INTERPOL believes."

"So you think they've got a backup plan?" William asked.

"Once we find out what it is, we can hand the ball over to NATO, mission accomplished," Mark revealed. "They can set up a military operation to intercept the shipment and shut the Russians down. With the US Chernobyl satellite and a couple of our nuclear subs, we just need to know where the Russians are planning to ship from. Obviously we can't cover the entire Atlantic. All we need is for you folks to narrow our search down."

"There's nothing more I can contribute," Lucretia insisted. "The Sicilians are out of the picture. I would not be surprised if the Mafia declares war on the Russian Mob."

"I need you to advise your superiors that we'll be relocating you to Toulouse to work undercover as backup for Shanahan. If you get made by the Corsicans, your story'll be that you broke ties with the Sicilians and are looking for work. You let them know you've got your Polish connections and you want to stay in the loop. You'll use your information about the incident with the Russians as bait. Don't give it up unless you have to, and they'll be able to verify it immediately. It should qualify you as soon as they do."

"Question," Shanahan was curt. "What makes us think the Corsicans are looking for a female driver? And what makes you think they won't make me if they discover she's keeping tabs on my activity?"

"The Poles and the Germans. Both of them know her credentials and they'll vouch for her. They're integral to the Russian network and won't be taken lightly. They still need someone to bring the shipment across the Alps. The Russians should still see this as a perfect gambit. I'm sure they'll insist that the Corsicans to guarantee she's solid, but that'll be taken care of."

"I don't know if I can take any more of this," Lucretia appeared distracted.

"I can fairly well assure you that you'll never have to go out again after this," Mark told her. "Parliament will almost certainly recommend you for a directorial position with our endorsement. Your bosses will hardly be in a position to deny you."

"Funny, I heard something similar sometime last year."

"You're MI6, it's a different situation. Plus you were given a choice."

"Aye, they offered me a ticket t'Paradise with forty dancing girls. What'd they tell you?"

"So we're all agreed to go another round?" Mark looked around at them.

"Yer sayin' if we find out where and when the big drop is comin', it's game over, is that what I'm hearin'?"

"I'd want to know the goods are en route before we call in the nuclear subs, but I'd say that's the gist of it."

"Good," Gawain leaned back with a grin. "I'll get me jumper cables out an' invite one of the Corsicans over for a pint. I should have a time and place for ye in a Belfast minute."

"It's just so wonderful to see you again. I can't believe we finally got connected."

"Aye, it's the luck o' th' Irish. They couldn't have kept us apart forever."

William barely concealed a smirk, allowing Fianna Hesher to enjoy the moment. He knew that Jack would have never referred to himself as Irish in most circumstances. The sexy blonde was elated when she found out that the two were arriving in Toulouse to meet her and Morgana that evening. Morgana was just as delighted that the guys were making time on their schedule, though she was more than happy that Fianna was getting to see Jack again after all this time.

He had purposely selected the boisterous, flash-lit club so that they would be lost in the crowd. Even so, they stood out in their semi-formal wear as the younger people were dressed casual at best. The only females wearing dresses appeared to have something to sell. The young men who cast glances at Morgana and Fianna were quickly dissuaded by withering stares from William and Jack. Most figured them for gangsters in their blazer jackets.

"So are you going to be in town tomorrow?" Morgana asked him as Jack was talking into Fianna's ear, making her giggle.

"No, we'll be hitting the road first thing in the morning," William replied. "I'm expecting to be wrapping things up in the next couple of days. If things go as planned, maybe we can spend a day on the Riviera."

"Now that would be worth the wait," her emerald eyes danced merrily. "I knew there wasn't much of a chance that we'd get to spend time together, but I couldn't resist giving it a try."

"I'm glad you did," he leaned over and kissed her cheek. "It's wonderful to be able to get away from the madness and spend time with you."

"I don't know how far away from the madness you got," Morgana quipped, nodding towards the dancers gyrating to the dub music beat.

"Excuse me, monsieur," a waiter placed a bucket of Dom Perignon on the table before them along with four glasses. "Compliments of a friend."

"And who'd that be?" William glanced about though carefully watching as the waiter uncorked the bottle.

"The gentleman in the suit there, in the far corner."

William peered furtively but was unable to discern anyone through the crowded dance floor and the flashing beams of colored light. He and the others failed to notice as the waiter innocuously raised his hand and pressed the stem of his watch with the other hand.

"Will you point him out to me when I'm by there?"

"Certainly, monsieur."

"Say, boyo," Jack came over and bent his head by William's ear. "I hate to seem anti-social, but Fianna and I have a bit of catchin' up to do, if ye know what I mean."

"It may not be the best idea," William was uncertain. "You know the Corsicans know I'm here in town. If they make you, they may put two and two together."

"I'm not all that concerned about the Corsicans at this stage of the game. They've got me, erm, marked as a righteous fellow, let's just say."

"Well, there'll be no dissuading you, I'm quite sure," William exhaled as Fianna was explaining herself to Morgana at his far left. "Do look out for a man in a suit by the entrance on the way out. He was supposedly the one who sent the champagne over."

"Aye, I'll give ye a buzz before the night's over. If it's anything that needs looking after, I'll take care of it."

"Do try not to saw anyone's head off under the spotlights, will you?"

"Not to worry," Jack patted his shoulder as he and Fianna walked off.

"I think we're alone now," Morgana leaned over towards him. "Do you think we might find a quieter place?"

"Why, certainly, love," he replied. "Montauban's about twenty minutes north of here. Perhaps we can take a ride out that way and find a cozy spot."

"That's the most romantic idea you've had in quite a while, mister."

"You do make it hard for a fellow to think of anything else."

They walked out arm-in-arm, though William was expecting to spot the benefactor who had sent the untouched bottle of champagne. He saw neither him nor the waiter who had brought the bucket over. The couple left the club and headed for the parking lot, though William was quite sure that there were questions to be answered in the foreseeable future.

The waiter watched from an alcove as William and Morgana left the club before activating the cell phone on his wristband. He transmitted the photos of the two couples to his counterparts in Naples, who were very interested in finding out more information about the women who had accompanied the two men. Moreover, they were intrigued as to the connection between these two men who appeared to be a very odd couple indeed.

Jack Gawain felt most self-satisfied just before noon the next day. He had brought Fianna to a local motel with a bottle of Irish whiskey and enjoyed a spirited evening of lovemaking with the lovely lass. They had not been together since last year, and he had not gotten the opportunity to consummate their relationship. This time it was different. She joined him in the shower when they checked into the room, and they ravished each other before toweling off and rejoining their lovefest in the bedroom. They exhausted each other numerous times before dropping off into sleep, then went at it again before and after showering the next morning. He spent a pretty penny having the cab bring her back to Toulouse before returning to Blagnac, but he considered it well worth it.

Even more exhilaration awaited him when he returned to Le Deauville Hotel. Darcy Callahan had rose early and had breakfast brought up to the room. Jack had only to pop his uneaten portion into the microwave and restore his energies before tackling the lingerie-clad woman onto the king-size bed.

"So you think you can spend all night on the town and just come back here and do whatever you want to me?" she muttered tantalizingly, tickling his nose with a strand of her dark hair as she gazed up into his eyes.

"Aye, that's pretty well what I've been fantasizin' about all night," he said before ruthlessly crushing his mouth down onto hers.

They exhausted each other three times before finally crashing out. It was the humming of his cell phone hours later that roused him from a glorious sleep. He picked it up and saw the icon of a tiny chess-type castle. It resembled the brand mark on his right arm. Next to it was *1800.*

"Don't tell me you have to leave again," Darcy was morose.

"Nay, not 'til this evening. Listen, why don't ye get prettied up an' we'll go out t'eat, then take a ride about town and see what the countryside's like? We're right near the Garonne River, I'm sure we'll find a few places to check out."

"That'd be fantastic!" she gushed, bounding across the bed and giving him a big hug and kiss. "Let me go take a shower and get ready. Thank you, thank you, thank you!"

He felt somewhat guilty about not having taken her out once since she arrived. Still, they were too close to Toulouse for comfort and he couldn't take a chance of having the Corsicans see them together. One of the first things he learned in business was to never let the competition get on to one's personal details. It was one of the quickest ways an enemy could strike in vengeance, and Jack had far too many enemies to afford himself a careless moment.

He had a rental car brought from the airport to the hotel, and they climbed into the BMW and headed towards the local market. They picked up a picnic basket, a bottle of wine, cheese and bread and a blanket before they continued on their way. They headed out to the river and cruised along the roadway, stopping for lunch and some heavy petting that went on for a couple of hours. It took them the rest of the day to return to the hotel, and Darcy considered it one of the best times of her life.

She had stars in her eyes as Jack went about preparing for the evening ahead. She was a fairly normal girl from Galveston, Texas, although having adopted the punk rock lifestyle. Meeting Jack last year was the most exciting thing that ever happened to her, even though he practically carjacked her after nearly having been murdered by assassins en route to Port Bolivar. He had entrusted her with more money than she had ever seen in her life, and the trip to Buckingham Palace for his award ceremony was the trip of a lifetime. Now there was all this. She knew that he might not have forgotten about Fianna Hesher, but she was determined that she would make him forget all about her rival somehow.

"All right, love, you be sure and stay inside. Don't go out unless it's a dire emergency. You can order anything ye need t'be brought up to you, okay?"

"You've got it, baby," she gave him a kiss before he headed out. "I'll be right here waiting for you."

She laid back in the bed and began dreamily flipping through channels on the TV, then rolled over to the nightstand and realized she was out of cigarettes. She was not a heavy smoker, enjoying one now and again like most people would indulge in a sip of wine. This was one of those times when she really wanted to have a smoke out on the balcony, She threw on a black workout suit and sneakers, then headed for the elevator to pick up a pack of smokes from the convenience store downstairs. She knew she could get an American magazine while she was there as well.

"Excuse me, mademoiselle, can you assist me?"

She took pity on the white-haired man at curbside, fumbling confusedly through a street map. He had an Italian accent and was dressed well, adjusting his gold-rimmed glasses on the tip of his nose. He was undoubtedly one of those who remained unaware of what bifocals were for.

"Sure, honey, what is it you're looking for?" she came up beside him, looking at his map.

At once she felt a powerful shock that caused her knees to buckle beneath her. Two pairs of arms grabbed hers on either side, keeping her on her feet long enough to shove her into a waiting vehicle. She was shoved over so that her huge breasts were as cushions against her knees, a cloth sack pulled over her head. She was then injected with a sedative that rendered her unconscious. It happened so quickly that no one even noticed as the black vehicle drove away.

Jack Gawain caught a cab to his hotel in Toulouse and found Chatillon's Citroen C4 Cactus awaiting. He hopped into the passenger seat as they cruised off. Chatillon sat behind him, two of his soldiers accompanying them on the trip.

"I hope there's not another branding party in store," Jack grunted.

"The day may come when the mark could save your life," Chatillon replied.

"I certainly feel like it saved my life the last time I was out there."

"Not to worry, my friend. This is going to be a most rewarding and profitable experience, I can assure you."

"That makes me feel a whole lot better."

They went through what Jack was now thinking of as the Citadel Car Wash, plowing through the manmade waterfall into the cavern where they parked the Citroen into the dark chambers. Only this time there were two squads of riflemen finishing up some drills, and were chanting some sort of military pledge before snapping to attention. The leader barked a command and they turned to their right in unison to march off into the depths of the catacombs.

"Real pretty," Jack smiled. "Can they fight?"

"Most of their enemies overseas wished they couldn't," Chatillon replied.

The four men lined up on the checkered floor facing the dais upon which the throne of the Black Queen sat. This time she arrived after they presented themselves, and nodded in acknowledging their bows before she spoke.

Again she wore the wide ceremonial dress, her headpiece and the shrouding veils, all as black as the shadows barely concealing her.

"As you know, the Russians are anxious to begin our shipments across Europe and over the Atlantic," she said crisply. "We have successfully eliminated the competition in exposing the weaknesses of the Sicilian network. Now all that is left is to cut the Corsican Mob out of the picture, and it will be our exclusive task to transport the weapons of mass destruction from Austria to the French coast."

"Erm, if I may, Your Highness," Jack spoke up, "I wasn't clear as to what kind of WMDs we're plannin' t'move."

"Gain!" Chatillon hissed.

"He has taken the mark, he has earned the right," the Queen responded. "Unfortunately we are not certain as to the nature of the weapon we will be transporting. What we do know is that the Ukrainian government did not surrender all of their WMDs to Russia as originally agreed upon. They kept a nuclear device and a biological weapon in case the Russians double-crossed them, as seems to be the case as we speak. What they did not anticipate was the emergence of Russian sympathizers who seized control of these classified storage facilities. It allowed the Spetznaz to take possession of the weapons. All that remains is for them to bring them across the eastern Ukrainian border into Poland, then across Germany into the Alps. Once they are in our possession, it is a matter of time before New York City becomes the site of the greatest devastation in the history of the world."

"What's in it for us, if I may ask, Your Highness?"

"The Russians are paying us fifty million dollars, which we are splitting between the organization and its members. You will have a quarter million US dollars transferred to the Swiss bank account of your choice upon completion of this operation."

"So am I understandin' that everyone gets paid, regardless of whether they participate or not?"

"This is how all of our transactions are processed. From the man on the field to the sentry on duty, we all profit equally. None are held in higher esteem than others."

"Sounds like I've landed in a pretty comfy place," Jack admitted.

"The Russians have been notified that we have confiscated the two previous shipments from the Sicilians and are holding them for safekeeping. At this time we are attempting to establish a link with the European Council. We wish to renegotiate their agreement to transport the weapons across the Atlantic. In the meantime, we intend to show the Russians that the Corsicans cannot be trusted with an operation of this magnitude. We will cause the Corsicans to fail in the last of the Russians' beta tests. Once again we will require your services in taking down the Corsicans."

"We will not fail, my Queen," Chatillon assured her.

The gravity of the situation was beginning to have an impact on Jack as they rode back to Toulouse. He had always been a take-charge guy back with the UDA in Belfast. It was the reason why he was so effective in America during Operation Blackout. If they let him off the leash he was able to shred his victims with no questions asked. Only this was the kind of chess game he always avoided. Direct confrontation was the best way to avoid getting stabbed in the back. It seemed as if the only way these people could operate was what the opponent's back was turned.

"I'm kinda wonderin' how it is yer so willin' t'take out yer fellow Corsicans t'get in closer with the Russians," Jack asked. "I'd just assumed if shite hit th' fan, y'know, like the Russians goin' up against NATO and such, ye might be wantin' some kind of solidarity."

"We've always wondered the same thing about the Protestants and the Catholics in Northern Ireland," Chatillon smiled. "Money and power turn brother against brother, children against parents. Crises, on the other hand, heals wounds easily and quickly. If the Russians threatened France, we would put aside our differences quickly, however temporarily."

"Aye, I getcha. Now, we knocked those Sicilians over quite handily. Those Corsicans, though, they've got t'be aware that we were hijackin' those shipments. Plus those two bitches and that guy we turned over t'have his balls flattened, ye know they went back and spilled the beans. If the Sicilians and the Corsicans're talkin' t' each other, the Corsicans'll have their radar up, to be sure. We might end up in a full-scale firefight this time."

"You saw those riflemen back there at the hideout. Plus we have you."

Jack got out in front of the hotel and waited in the lobby until the Corsicans were out of sight. He then waved down a cab and headed back to Blagnac. He had not been spending much time at his room at the Hotel de France, stopping by to change clothes at best. He spent most of his time at Le Deauville with Darcy, and was irked when he arrived to find she was not there. He tried to reach her on her cell phone but got no answer. He hoped she had not done anything stupid, but had no time to dwell on it. He decided to call Six and set up a meet with William Shanahan.

"He wants to see you too," Six informed him. "Access the MI6 website for time and place."

Jack cursed as he changed into a black sweatshirt and cargo pants. He had little patience for all these secret agent bollocks. He was well aware that there was enough high-tech equipment out there to pick off any form of communication, but they had to know where to look. So far the bad guys didn't seem to have a clue. At any rate, he was not going to begin quibbling with Six. If the sorry bastard wanted to continue playing switchboard operator, it was fine with him.

"How now, boyo," Jack phoned the number on the website after logging off. They had nagged him incessantly to log off his PC as soon as he got off the MI6 website to avoid anyone dropping a virus on him. "About time they gave up yer number."

"I'll come to meet you in a half hour."

"Ye know where I am?"

"I ran into Darcy a couple of days ago. It wasn't hard to figure out."

"Shite," Jack hissed before the line went dead.

He went down to the lobby and decided to have a smoke outside while waiting for Shanahan. He hadn't taken a couple of drags before he felt a light poke in the back.

"Sneaky of ye, fella," Jack turned to face him.

"Better tweak your radar. C'mon, let's walk."

"So, what's new by you?" Jack asked, relishing the view of the classy French boulevard.

"Fianna's missing."

"What, again?" he was exasperated, remembering her unwitting sojourn with Enrique Chupacabra during Operation Blackout last year. "How'd the silly twit get tangled up this time?"

"She flew out with Morgana. They took some vacation time after getting tipped off by that Homeland Security connection of theirs. I didn't tell you because I didn't want you trying anything foolish."

"Well, don't ye think ye should be confrontin' me when questionin' me judgment?"

"That's the first order of business. What in hell were you thinking by bringing Darcy out here?"

"I needed cash. Look, we went over this last year in New York. You people put me out on th' field, representin' meself as a wiseguy, an' ye give me a piece of plastic for pocket money. Street guys don't use plastic, I told ye that after I stuck up that crack house in Harlem. I had a stash layin' up with Darcy after I took out that crack house in Liberty City back there in Florida. I figured I'd kill two birds with one stone by flyin' her out. If I knew ye were havin' Fianna out, I might've just have her wire it along."

"When's the last time you saw Darcy?"

"Aye, she's missin'. It must've been the Italians, I'll look into it. Now, are you goin' out with those Corsicans of yours? I think ye need t'stay off the field for a bit. It may start gettin' rough out there."

"How deep are you in with your Corsicans?"

"Real deep. I'm not askin' ye, I'm tellin' ye. Don't go out if they ask ye. Tell 'em that European Council's got a rule or somethin'."

"I appreciate your concern. Rest assured I'm not quite new to this game. I was with the SAS, you remember."

"Aye, well, sometimes ye come across as a bit naïve, Gummo, not t'be insultin'."

"I've been thinking the same thing of you, fellow. Did you bring your women onto the field with you when you were working with the UDA?"

"Sometimes they were loadin' the guns whilst we were firin'. Look, if I spill the beans ye might feel beholden t'tip off O'Shaughnessy, and I can't have it. We're this close t' cornerin' the Russians. I just don't want ye t'end up in a jackpot if it's unnecessary."

"I'm almost speechless over your sudden concern. All right, let's play a couple of cards here. I know the Sicilians are just about out of the picture."

"They *are* out. I held the door for 'em."

"Nice to know. Actually I don't get involved until the shipment's ready to launch. I'm quite sure O'Shaughnessy'll spring the trap then."

"Reason with me, boyo. If these smugglers are baitin' and switchin' each other all over the map, what makes ye think they won't pull it on you?"

"Why would they? They believe I'm their only hope in avoiding the Yanks' Chernobyl satellite, not to mention Her Majesty's submarines."

"Aye, but ye haven't proven yerself sound. Don't forget, yer still th' last man who saw Emiliano Murra alive. He was a mid-management man. Ye don't think it's quite under th' bridge yet, do ye?"

"That's the risk we take. You can't win if you don't play. As we say in the SAS, who dares wins."

"As I used t'say in the UDA, ye cheat t'win, ye win t'cheat. Tell me, William, what d'ye have on the girl?"

"Pretty complicated," William said as they crossed the street, continuing their stroll away from the hotel. "Let me see if I can make it simple. INTERPOL hasn't worked right since the Allies took it back from the Nazis after the War. Since the EU was established, alongside EUROPOL it grew some teeth. Still, it's not like in the UK where the Crown supersedes the member nations. It's more like the US where the States can argue with the Federal Government. INTERPOL's almost like an independent contractor. Lucretia Carcosa's somewhat of a subcontractor."

"Like me, eh?"

"You got it. Anyway, I talked to Joe Bieber, the CIA fellow. He's the one who checked her out. They show her having worked a couple of ops in Poland, but that's about it."

"Someone needs to get her out of th' game. She escaped gettin' her tits mashed by a cunt hair. She's not up for this game, fella. Matter of fact, as I said, I think you'd better sit this one out as well. This is gonna start gettin' ugly."

"Tell you what. Why don't we come clean with one another and see if we can work something out between us?"

"I can't spill everything for a number of reasons. But I can sit down with ye an' figure out a game plan."

"All right. I've got my ride at the Four Seasons. I'll meet you here in ten minutes. We'll ride out to Montauban and sort things out."

"What'll it be then, eh?"

"I'd rather not do it your way this time," Jean-Paul Chatillon stared through his infra-red binoculars at the target site across the street from the darkened warehouse where they sat. "In this particular instance, however, I don't see any other options."

The man called Jack Gain took the binoculars and peered out onto the deserted street. There was a nondescript white van with the words 'The Curio Shop' in Edwardian script on its side parked at the foot of an antiquated girder bridge crossing a small creek. A black van had just turned onto the narrow street and paused for a while before flashing its headlights. The white van hit its emergency lights, and the black van began rolling slowly towards the delivery truck.

"All right, let's do it," Jack said.

There were four men accompanying Jack and Chatillon, all dressed in black fatigues. About a half hour ago, they had rolled up the metal door of the rental property and replaced it with a cleverly designed canvas painted to look like the door itself. As soon as the black vehicle had parked behind the white van, the Corsicans' SUV ripped through the canvas and rolled onto the street facing parallel to the smugglers. It caused the occupants of the white van to rush back towards the vehicle to retrieve their own weapons. Having the advantage, the Citadel mercenaries rushed the van with their Uzis blazing. In less than a minute, the Corsicans were sprawled across the pavement, blood oozing from their corpses.

"Shoot the tires on the driver side!" Jack yelled at one of the mercs. The gunman let loose a burst that blew out the tires. It caused the van to drop to its left, bouncing on its rims and crashing through the guardrail. They watched as it tumbled down the steep gully and splash into the creek.

Suddenly the tires of a police vehicle squealed as it spun around the corner, its strobe lights flashing as it slammed to a halt. The officers began drawing their weapons as they hopped out of the vehicle. Only they were confronted by Jack, who opened up on them with Uzi fire and cut them down in their tracks. Before the mercs could react, Jack spun around and raked them with automatic fire. Chatillon stared in horror as his comrades dropped to the pavement, blood spilling across the cobblestoned road. He was caught entirely off-guard as Jack rushed up to him and smashed him across the jaw, dropping him to the ground.

As if on cue, a black vehicle sped around the corner, narrowly managing to avoid tail-ending the patrol car. William Shanahan screeched to a halt amidst the bodies sprawled over the street as Jack hauled Chatillon to his feet.

"What is this?" William stared about in disbelief. "Did you do all this, you crazy bastard?"

"Aye, an' ye'd better get movin' unless ye wanna stick around an' pay for it," Jack said, puling open the back door and shoving Chatillon in ahead of him.

With that, William hit the gas and they streaked across the bridge into the night.

Chapter Eight

Shanahan remembered back when he was a lieutenant in Baghdad shortly after Desert Storm. He was with a recon team who lost two members to a car bomb, the second that went off in a crowded bazaar within an hour in different parts of the city. They dragged a suspect into a blast-damaged storefront after a bystander spotted him activating a cell phone an instant before the explosion. A member beat him with a length of barbed wire he carried for such occasions. Upon pouring lye on the man's wounds, they were told the location of a third car bomb. The resulting evacuation saved countless lives.

He tried to remind himself of that as Gawain applied the tips of a hot wire to a chain wrapped around Jean-Paul Chatillon's testicles. The Citadel captain was hanging from an overhead pipe the basement of a construction site outside of Innsbruck. The man screamed until his voice broke, nearly passing out from the excruciating pain.

"All right, I'll ask ye again. Who is the Black Queen?"

"That's enough, Jack," Shanahan interceded. "You've popped him twice already. If he knew he would've told you. If you pop him again he may go into shock."

"Well, then, he'll be like Aladdin's lamp," Gawain grinned wickedly. He held the hot wire away from himself as it was still hooked up to the car battery. "Ye can have him answer one more question."

"Find out about his Russian connection. How are they contacting the Russians?"

"Gain, how could you do this?" Chatillon gasped, blood running from a gash where he had nearly bitten through his lip. "The Queen will never stop looking for you. Ever. You were one of us. How could you?"

"Ye shouldn't have brought that up," Gawain waved the hot wires menacingly.

"What's he talking about?"

"A little souvenir I picked up, th' price of admission," Gawain dropped the hot wires, pulling his shirt off halfway and revealing the brand on his right arm.

"Looks rather painful," Shanahan noted.

"Aye, not somethin' ye'd wave yer hand in class for. Aw reet, ye heard th' man. How d'we get in touch with the Russians?"

"How do I know you won't kill me after I tell you?"

"How do ye know I will? Besides, this fella here's a British Boy Scout of sorts. He'd probably be upset with me if I did ye in."

"Everything is done over the Internet. They have a secure website and all the e-mails are encrypted. They are the ones who normally initiate contact, and they dictate terms. They would be very suspicious if I contacted them."

"We've got their shipment, and you've got th' first two we picked off. Tell 'em ye got waylaid, an' ye wanna turn everything in because INTERPOL's onto ye."

"That's not how it worked out," Chatillon gasped, his hands turning blue from the loss of circulation as they were chained over his head. "We returned the first two shipments in order to have the Sicilians excluded from the deal. It was an act of good faith on our part. If I tell them the Citadel was double-crossed, they'll know we were compromised. They'll smell a trap."

"Tell them it was the European Council," Shanahan suggested. "You'll say the Council is trying to leverage you out of the deal and you need advice. Tell them you survived the ambush but you're concerned that the Council may have broken your security codes."

"I'll try," Chatillon managed. "Just let me down, for god's sake."

Gawain dutifully pulled a stool up behind Chatillon and popped the chain loose from the overhead winch. The merc leader collapsed to the cement floor in a heap.

"Okay, here's the deal. You help us out and I'll have you sent to London after we're done. I can have them put you in a supergrass program as an informer. Either that or I'll turn you over to the Yanks as a terrorist. You'll probably be at Guantanamo Bay sometime tomorrow. You could end up there for the rest of your life," Shanahan said flatly.

"That sounds like a feckin' waste o' th' American taxpayers' money," Gawain pulled his Glock, flipped the safety and pressed the barrel against Chatillon's head.

"No," Chatillon begged. "Please."

"That won't be necessary," Shanahan insisted. "Jean-Paul, welcome to the team."

Gilles Marotte found himself on the horns of a dilemma as his Family was buffeted by the aftershock of the collapsed arms deal with the Russians. Although the Sicilian Mob had borne the Russians' wrath over the foiled transports, the most recent attack brought the capabilities of the Corsican Mob into question. From all accounts, it sounded like the work of the rogue Citadel mercenaries. Only they had no solid evidence as yet and had gotten no feedback from the Russians when they communicated their suspicions.

He knew that the deal was growing shakier by each passing day. Obviously the Citadel was trying to seize control of the network by eliminating the Sicilians, and now the Corsicans. Marotte had made a deal with the couriers, Pinzone and Montesano, but they were nearly killed when the hijackers forced their delivery truck off a bridge into a creek. Now they were here to handle a different assignment today: the disposal of the kidnapped lady friends of Jack Gain.

News had spread throughout the underworld of Gain's meeting with Danny Di Benedetto in Rome and the rejected offer to sell the Russian arms back to the Sicilians. Most likely Gain and the Citadel were the ones who hijacked the RPG-7s from Marotte's smugglers.

There was now the problem of assuaging William Bruce and the European Council, who were growing skeptical with the continuous delays. Marotte could not deny the fact that the Corsican-Sicilian connection was appearing as increasingly unreliable. Now that the Sicilians were virtually out of the picture, the shadow of doubt was being cast on the Corsicans.

He disliked having to deal with women, but so far they appeared to be the strongest leak in a rusty chain. Lucinda Montesano had curried favor with Don Cesare in Sicily, and had been paired with the Mob's top female assassin. They defected to the Corsican Mob after escaping death at the hands of the Russians in Austria. Only now they had narrowly cheated fate after a second encounter with the Citadel. Marotte decided he would give them this task to test their resolve. It would provide them with a respite while he mended the relationship with the Russians.

The more he admired the Russian network, the more of an embarrassment the Corsican-Sicilian connection was. The special forces operatives used the Russian Mob as middlemen. The gangsters acted as couriers in communicating with the Poles and the Germans. The Russian commandos only came out when necessary, as they did when they punished Vito Garibaldi for falling into the Citadel's trap. They let the Corsicans know it was a warning for all who compromised their mission. Only now he was uncertain whether the Corsicans would be held as an example to others. Gilles Marotte would do his utmost to prevent it from happening.

"This creates an awkward position for us all. If these women are not returned, INTERPOL will not rest until they are found. Consider the cost, monsieur."

Concetta Pinzone sat with him in the great hall of his mansion that morning. He had been switching back and forth from the BBC to *Al Jazeera* on his wide-screen plasma TV before she arrived. Photos of Fianna Hesher and Darcy Callahan were plastered all over the news as it was announced that the women had possibly been kidnapped by terrorists in Southern France. This was an unforeseen situation that resulted in calls from all his fellow Mob leaders. Marotte had planned to use the women as leverage in case Jack Gain and the Citadel acted against him. Now everyone was pleading with him to discard his ace in the hole. He was greatly reluctant to do so, but the political pressure was proving unbearable.

"This is impossible," Marotte shook his head. "This entire operation is turning to shit. First the Sicilians, now us. I have always doubted the resiliency of the Sicilian Mob, ever since the FBI began crushing their operations in America. More and more of their soldiers are becoming informers, breaking our code of honor to save themselves. If they are making deals so easily with the police, I have to ask myself how much easier it is to make deals with the Citadel for promises of fortune?"

"Do you feel the Corsicans are also selling out, betraying confidences?"

"No, I believe that Jack Gain and his men have gotten detailed information about the operation that is causing these problems. We are going to have to wipe the slate clean and start over. All of the planned routes throughout Southern Europe must be cancelled. We will have to meet with the Russians and make a new plan. Otherwise the Citadel will continue to ambush our couriers and cause the Russians to cancel the deal. We will lose millions if that happens."

"Lucinda is outside guarding the two women. Your soldiers await downstairs to drive us to Palermo. Are you sure this is what you want?"

"I see little choice in the matter. If we kill them and dispose of the bodies, the search will be relentless. We already have all the information about Gain that we could obtain. They said he went by the name of Jack Gawain in England and was decorated in Buckingham Palace along with a man named William Shanahan. Our connections turn up nothing on either of them. Obviously he has worked with MI6, which is probably why the Citadel recruited him. The women are of no further use to us. Take them to Palermo and drop them off outside of town somewhere. When you return, we will discuss cutting ties with the Sicilians and improving relations with the Russians."

"If this is what you wish, then I will handle it for you."

"Very good, Concetta. We will visit again soon."

"I don't think so," she said, opening her purse as she rose from her chair.

"What?"

Concetta pulled a Beretta from her bag and pointed it at Marotte's head.

"Don Masseroli sends his regards."

She then fired a shot, hitting him between the eyes.

Concetta was wearing a wire, which signaled the soldiers positioned around the mansion to spring into action. There were men on motorcycles armed with RPG-7s on each side of the estate. They gunned their engines and roared onto the property, readying the launchers and firing grenades into each side of the building. Marotte's bodyguards were caught off-guard, and the resulting explosions threw the squad into a panic. The housekeeping staff were screaming and running in all directions as the wounded crawled to escape the flaming mansion. No one was in position to react to the helicopter that descended over the rooftop to drop its rope ladder.

"Move it, you stupid bitches!" Concetta shoved the captives towards a stairwell leading to the emergency corridor. Lucinda held the door open and guided the handcuffed women up the staircase to the roof entrance. Fianna and Darcy were terrified as they were herded towards the rope ladder, but realized it was their only chance of escape. They trembled with fear as they climbed the ladder and were pulled into the helicopter. Lucinda and Concetta followed, and soon the chopper flew off into the clouds.

It was the beginning of a Sicilian-Corsican mob war that would claim dozens of lives in the months ahead.

"So the Corsicans are also out of the picture."

"They appear incapable of completing their assignments. I believe it is time to truly test their mettle, as we did with the Sicilians. If they are unable to negotiate the test, then we will go ahead with our alternate plan. It is becoming more obvious that we cannot rely on these criminal organizations. It takes professionals to do professional jobs. This is why we may end up placing all our trust on the Citadel."

"I agree, Captain. Tell me how you wish to proceed."

Lieutenant Glazunov was one of Captain Rudenko's most trusted subordinates. Together they successfully ended the Chechen terror crisis in Beslan in 2004 before serving tours in Dagestan in hunting down Islamic terror gangs. The Federal Security Service of Russia had selected this Spetznaz team and told them this mission officially never existed. There was no official record of a nuclear warhead or a chemical warhead having been reclaimed from a secret Ukrainian storage facility. The Government had no record of AK-47s and RPG-7s being reclaimed from Ukrainian armories and shipped out of the country. Whatever happened from here would be denied at the highest levels. Rudenko was glad to accept the responsibility.

"We will be targeting the French ports of Brest and Bayonne," Rudenko pointed to a map of France in the small office in the warehouse along the outskirts of Montauban. "One of these will be a ruse to deceive the INTERPOL agents on our trail. The other will be the actual shipment destined for New York City. In order to ensure the utmost security, I will not reveal the delivery route to either squad until the last minute. You will be personally supervising the shipment of the nuclear device. The Ukrainians will be led by Lieutenant Maklakov in transporting the thermobaric bomb. We are quite certain that INTERPOL may be able to intercept one of the shipments, but not both. The one that makes it through will bring about the end of the myth of American invincibility."

The thermobaric device yielded the equivalent of forty-four tons of TNT that included seven tons of a sophisticated explosive compound. It generated a sustained blast wave of higher temperatures than other eight-ton devices of similar size. It would be transported on an eighteen-wheel truck to the designated port where it would be loaded onto one of the European Council's cargo ships. The smaller nuclear device would be concealed in an oil barrel. If both shipments were to elude the INTERPOL network, the thermobaric weapon would be relocated to the Washington DC area.

"I only question the prudence of leaving the possibility of having one of the weapons seized to chance. I can assure you, Captain, if you gave me as much as a week, I could hunt down this Citadel and end this threat once and for all."

"Request denied. My dear Glazunov, There is no time to indulge ourselves in such ventures. NATO is placing enormous pressure in Mother Russia to give up its quest to reunite the nations of our former Soviet Union. The Government is losing billions of dollars every week as the US and its allies tighten the economic noose around our neck. We must establish our terror option before the nations of the world. If the thermobaric bomb is intercepted, it will send a wave of panic around the globe. How can you threaten to attack your neighbor when your house is about to explode? They will drop everything to ensure their own national security. This will allow our leaders to continue with their plan."

"I like the idea of having our WMDs near New York and Washington. However, detonating a nuke in New York City will permanently cripple our enemies. I will rest assured in your wisdom as always."

"This is why I am placing the nuclear device in your charge. We can afford to lose the thermobaric bomb. The nuclear bomb will change the course of history. In this you must not fail."

"You have my word of honor. This mission will not fail."

The port of Brest was the most accessible of ports for ships arriving from the Americas due to its salient position on the French coast. Its protected location allowed it to receive an aircraft carrier, the USS Nimitz, in years past. And so it was that the eighteen-wheeler pulling onto the waterfront area drew no undue attention en route to its scheduled destination. The driver patiently made his way along the driveways and waited until he approached Pier 13, where he took his time in maneuvering towards the loading dock.

The man in the passenger seat watched as a man opened the warehouse door and signaled the driver into the bay. The driver began backing the truck into a semi-circle as his partner hopped down from the cab. A second figure emerged from the warehouse and descended the concrete stairs to the left of the loading dock. The man from the truck sauntered over and greeted his counterpart.

"Another equal opportunity employer," the man spoke French with an Eastern European accent. "There was a time when the only time you saw women was when you left to do a job and when you got back home."

"Times have changed, my friend. Are the two of you all that was needed to move this freight?" the woman asked as the truck backed into the loading area.

"Of course not. We take our own precautions," he replied. As if on cue, the overhead door of the truck rolled open and four men armed with AK-47s clambered from within. They were greeted by the men in the warehouse who came out to meet the arriving crew.

"Do your men intend to unload the truck with AKs on their backs?" she wondered. "If a safety catch flips, someone could get hurt."

"We're just making everything is in order. There have been quite a few screwups since this operation began. We want to make sure everyone is who they say they are before they begin unpacking."

The smuggler turned toward the dock and was startled by a beam of light that flashed from the night sky and illuminated the truck. He started to move but felt a hand grab his collar and a cold gun barrel pressing against his chin. They watched as the helicopter descended upon the pier and unmarked cars began swarming over the area.

"INTERPOL, don't move," Lucretia Carcosa hissed. "Down on your knees, now."

"This will cost you your job, you stupid bitch," the Ukrainian laughed as he put his hands behind his head. "Do you think we were sent here by a bunch of idiots?"

"No, I think they sent a bunch of idiots who will be doing ten to twenty for arms smuggling," she said as she cuffed his wrists behind his back before shoving him face first to the asphalt. She used the back of his neck as a stepping stone, walking toward her fellow agents who were rushing over to collect the trucker.

"This doesn't look good," a senior agent came over and offered her a cigarette which she declined. "These bastards are carrying some kind of diplomatic papers for the firearms. This one'll go over our heads if we come up empty inside the truck."

"Why would you say that?"

"These Russians are playing this one perfectly," the agent exhaled a stream of smoke. "Have you considered the fact that the Citadel has countered their every move thus far? I'm starting to think they've jockeyed into position as a quality control team. If they convince the Russians that this deal will not happen without them, logic would dictate that they will be the ones to complete the major shipments."

"They suckered us," another agent came over to them after about ten minutes of unloading. "There's nothing but plumbing supplies inside. Most of it is heavy pipeline without caps. It's almost as if they wanted us to see there's nothing inside. The wooden crates are barely sealed."

"Isn't there anything we can do to send them to Guantanamo?" Lucretia insisted.

"No, the best we'll get is sticking them in that shithole in Brest until the Russian Embassy springs them. They'll probably be on their way back to the Ukraine by tomorrow night."

"Disgusting," she shook her head.

"Who knows, maybe the Brits will have better luck."

"The Brits?"

"Haven't you heard? They're pulling one last sting operation before they close it down. The word is that they are handing it off now that the Sicilians and the Corsicans have been taken out of the game. They believe the Russians will abort the operation rather than place all their trust in some untested mercenary outfit. It's do or die for the Citadel, and I don't think they are going to make it."

Further south along the French coast, a delivery truck was rumbling toward the Bayonne harbor. It was a traditional stopover for boats crossing the Gulf of Biscay from the UK to the Iberian Peninsula. The traffic here was not as heavy as at the Brest seaport, and there were less security concerns due to its reputation as a recreational port. Together with the breaking news over the INTERPOL operation at Brest, the activity at Bayonne seemed as if it would slip under the radar altogether.

The team of smugglers emerged from the shadows along the pier where the cargo ship was docked. It was an eight-man team carrying Uzis at their sides as they came up to meet the truck crew. They also carried automatic weapons, and Lieutenant Glazunov stepped forth to confront the man known as William Bruce.

"At last we meet," Glazunov exchanged handshakes. "It is unfortunate that this transaction has been delayed for so long. There were unexpected problems along the network, but it seems we have been able to eliminate them. I trust your people are prepared to take possession and bring this to our associates in New York City."

"Yes we are. Have you brought both devices?"

"No, one of the products is being kept here. My superiors have decided they would be of better use elsewhere."

"I was not notified. Will we still be getting paid the amount we agreed upon?"

"Most certainly. Five million American dollars will be electronically transferred to your Swiss bank account as soon as your ship leaves this dock. The remaining five million will be transferred as soon as our associates confirm receipt of the delivery in New York."

"Excellent. My only regret is that we are being kept out of the loop as regards the second device. I would hope that this has nothing to do with the Citadel. My superiors would be disappointed to think you have placed your confidence in a rival organization."

"As a matter of fact, we have hired the Citadel to replace the gangsters we had originally hired to bring our shipments across France. They will ensure the timely delivery of our armaments from here on in."

"There's not going to be any other shipments. That truck of yours contains a nuclear device."

"Where did you get that information?" Glazunov stared at him. "We told your Corsican contacts we were supplying arms to militants in the US to destabilize their economy. Nothing was mentioned about WMDs."

"Every bucket has leaks, and we've found all of yours. You're under arrest, Glazunov."

At once William's companions trained their Uzis on the Russians, catching them flatfooted. They slowly placed their weapons on the ground and held their hands in the air. Just as on the dock in Brest, a fleet of cars began rolling onto the driveway which was being illuminated by an overhead spotlight from a descending helicopter.

"You clever bastard," Glazunov smirked. "The European Council was a front. You've been conning the Corsican Mob for over a year."

"Not just them," William said curtly as a squad of MI6 agents exited their vehicles and headed towards the Russians. "Our Council has connections with every gang in Europe, including the Russian Mob. Not that the information will do you much good. You'll be on the next flight to Guantanamo in a few hours."

There was a row of trailer-sized storage containers at the far end of the dock. Jack Gawain and Jean-Paul Chatillon watched from inside one of the metal boxes. Chatillon's wrists were cuffed behind his back, while Gawain stood guard with an Uzi. They were able to hear the entire conversation with a receiver tuned in to the wire Shanahan was wearing. It was similar to the ones the intercept team leaders were using.

"Well, boyo, it looks like our Citadel friends stayed clear of this cluster feck, eh?" Gawain smiled, peering out at the activity on the dock.

"What will happen to me now?" Chatillon muttered.

"As Gummo said, they can get ye a job as a double agent. Unless, of course, ye'd rather take up residence in Guantanamo. I hear it's not th' best choice of beach property."

"Why would you betray us, Jack? We accepted you as a brother. You could have become a very rich man. You are being used by these people, you must realize that."

"You'd never understand, fella," Gawain glanced at Chatillon. "Th' reason I joined the UDA was for God and country. Th' money part was all gravy. You and yours, ye pledge allegiance t' yer Queen an' yer brotherhood, but deep down ye know yer just a band of thieves. I fight for a cause. God and country, y'see."

"That's what they've brainwashed you to believe."

"Aye, well, it helps me sleep at night."

"You sleep because you have no conscience. You're a serial killer, a mass murderer."

"And a decorated one at that."

Suddenly there was a great roar that descended over the loading dock. Gawain looked out and saw a great explosion as the MI6 helicopter erupted into a ball of flames. He looked up from the slit in the wall of the metal container and could see a Dassault Mirage IIIV hovering over the dock, raining fire down on the vehicles and the fleeing agents. It was the prototype of the VTOL[1] crafts that preceded the British Harrier aircraft. It had the firepower and flight capability of a fighter jet, though had the ability to hover like a helicopter. Its M134 miniguns featured six barrels firing six thousand 7.62mm rounds per minute. The six cars on the dock were blown apart in seconds, the agents ripped to shreds by the armor-piercing shells.

Gawain continued to watch as a rope was lowered along with the Mirage. Four men in black descended and rushed to the delivery truck, shooting the men inside before pulling a hooked cable inside the van. They swiftly clambered out and gave a signal, at which point the Mirage shifted position in order to pull the tethered object from the truck. Gawain could see a huge barrel bouncing along the pavement at the end of the cable. The Mirage held its position until the soldiers could

1. vertical take-off and landing

access the rope and climb back into the aircraft. With that, the plane rose into the sky before dipping slightly and soaring away.

"That was the Citadel, wasn't it?" Gawain pulled his Glock from his waistband.

"I couldn't have possibly known," Chatillon gasped. "I've been with you all this time. Apparently the plans were altered."

"Son of a bitch," Gawain snarled, firing a shot between Chatillon's eyes as his brains spurted across the shipping container. Gawain threw the door open and raced onto the dock where he found Shanahan trying to pull himself into a sitting position.

"Well, boyo, ye've looked better."

"I'm hit," Shanahan's bloodied hand held a set of keys. "I parked my car off on that side. I rented a room just outside of town."

"Well, looks like we'll need to stop for band-aids. I can pick up a couple of pints if ye like."

"If you don't get a move on, you'll be drinking them by yourself."

"Don't sweat it, fella. I've seen a lot worse. Ye'll be fine. Now I need t'haul ye up, are ye ready? Put yer arm around me neck. Push yerself as best ye can."

Shanahan hissed, barely managing not to cry out from the pain. Gawain noticed the blood dripping behind them as they hobbled nearly thirty yards to the car parked along the road. He opened the door and helped Shanahan in before William fell unconscious.

Chapter Nine

The world watched in horror as a video of the Black Queen was broadcast by the BBC and *Al Jazeera* after being forwarded from the Office of Cuba Broadcasting in Havana. The OCB refused to divulge the origin of the video that was transmitted to them, but verified that the senders identified themselves as the Citadel.

"Our organization has recently intercepted the delivery of weapons of mass destruction that were being smuggled from the Ukraine by criminal organizations hired by elements of the Russian Army known as the Spetznaz," she spoke deliberately, her voice garbled and her image distorted. "These weapons were destined for New York City to be placed in the hands of terrorist groups. There can be no doubt that our actions have saved thousands, perhaps millions of lives. Yet our benevolence does come at a price. In order to ensure the safe transfer of these weapons to members of NATO so that they no longer present a threat to the people of the US, we ask a fee of one billion dollars to be paid to a designated Swiss bank account. If this transaction is not processed within seventy-two hours, we will detonate the first of these weapons in a major European capitol. We will then provide a second grace period, after which we will be forced to detonate the nuclear device on American soil. We implore the people of the European Union and the United States of America: do not allow your leaders to test our resolve in this matter."

"Y'see, Gummo, I'll have t'go an' handle this meself," Gawain said as he leaned back in the chair by the small table in the motel room outside of Bayonne.

"You can't go alone. You can't do this without checking with Six. Lives are at stake," Shanahan managed, barely able to endure the burning pain in his left arm and leg. Gawain had dug the bullets out and treated them with medical supplies he obtained at gunpoint at a local store.

"An' what'll you do, act as a distraction while I'm out workin'?" Gawain chuckled, turning down the volume on the TV with the remote control. "Maybe if we're bein' chased, I can toss ye from th' car an' hope they crash tryin' t'avoid ye."

"I can drive. You may need a getaway. Plus I can call Six if you're arrested or captured."

"Y'see, boyo, that's yer problem. The last Boy Scout. Ye don't know when t'quit. Yer about a pint short, y'know. If I gave two shites about ye, I'd dump ye off in front of a hospital. Plus those holes in ye are liable t'get infected, an' then yer in a world of shite, don't ye know."

"My only concern would be if they bagged you and tagged you and MI6 didn't claim you," Shanahan managed, his left eye blackened from falling head first to the pavement after getting shot. "At least I could make sure they shipped you back to Shankill Road for a proper send-off."

"Feckin' Boy Scout," Gawain shook his head. "Okay, let's sort this out. That feckin' Queen is gonna make a grandstand play here. She'll be plannin' t'make a move that'll go down in history. A bitch who sits herself on a throne in front of her gang wouldn't settle for less. Plus the crew's too seasoned to make any stupid moves. They're not gonna try t'cross borders with a WMD. Think about it, boyo. I say they're goin' for th' Eiffel Tower."

"No chance," Shanahan sipped from the straw in his canister of mint-flavored tea. "Those kind of targets'll be guarded to the max. How're they gonna bring an oil drum within a mile of it?"

"Oil drum, my arse. This one's th' thermobaric bomb. This'll be delivered by that Harrier, or whatever th' feck th' frogs call theirs."

"The French Air Force'll be swarming the skies over Paris. There'd be no chance."

"An' what'll they do, get into a dogfight in the skies above Paris?" Gawain sneered. "Once they pick it up, they'll order it t'land. They're not gonna expect it t'have vertical capability. They'll swing that bomb in like a wrecking ball, an' they'll negotiate from wherever it sticks."

"You make it sound pretty simple."

"I'm lookin' at it through th' eyes of desperate men who'll take whatever they can get."

"So when do you want to make your move?"

"Th' Queen may be a pompous bitch, but she's not stupid. She's not gonna wait seventy-two hours t'let them get set. We're about six hours from Paris. I'm about ready t'pack an' take off, boyo. Are ye gonna be ready to hang?"

"Give me a couple of minutes to pull my clothes on, and I'm ready to go."

"Say, that reminds me. When're we goin' after Fianna and Darcy?"

"Nukes first, I'd say."

"Good. Ye can explain it to those two twits when we spring 'em."

The member nations of NATO were of like mind with Jack Gawain. After issuing dire threats to the Kremlin, they scheduled emergency meetings in every capitol city to determine their next course of action. The surviving members of the MI6 team that was ambushed by the Citadel in Bayonne confirmed that the renegade Legionnaires were probably sequestered somewhere in France. It was unlikely that they would have intruded upon the airspace of a neighboring country after surviving the odds as they did in Bayonne.

Mark O'Shaughnessy was among those summoned to the upper-echelon security meeting at the Palais Bourbon in Paris that morning. He had been hard-pressed by Parliament members as well as the INTERPOL and EUROPOL administrators who had organized the summit. He was among those who felt that England's security matters were sacrosanct, and was noticeably irritable in being called to question by those in attendance.

"The agents assigned to this operation are deep undercover," O'Shaughnessy replied testily to the EUROPOL inquiry as to MI6's updated intel. "I'm quite sure my American colleague can elaborate as to what that entails. My people have either infiltrated the gang or are holding the leash on those inside. I will not take personal responsibility for giving up information that may result in one of my operatives taking a bullet to the head."

"We doubt that the situation is as dire as you perceive it to be," the representative of the DCRI[1] was patronizing. "If I may be so presumptuous, you are among your peers here. Unless, of course, that is a category reserved for your so-called Cousins in Langley."

"The United States of America doesn't play favorites, our colleagues in INTERPOL and EUROPOL are well aware of that," Joe Bieber spoke up. "We stand shoulder-to-shoulder with every member nation to annihilate these terror threats wherever they exist. However, I have to concur with Colonel O'Shaughnessy in placing the safety of his operatives as a primary concern."

"These bastards have threatened to detonate a WMD on European soil," the representative from DPSD[2] was vehement. "If these weapons were in England or America, I think the safety of your operatives would be of less consequence."

"I won't even dignify that remark," O'Shaughnessy blustered. "A threat to one is a threat to all. That is the only reason why we are here."

"Gentlemen, why are we creating arguments that distract us from the crisis at hand?" Bieber beseeched them. "It would stand to reason that our French colleagues would have far more information about the Citadel than we possibly could. We were told by MI6 that these

---

1. Central Directorate of Interior Intelligence
2. Directorate for Defense Protection and Security

people are hardcore commandos, possibly Foreign Legion or COS[3]. Surely you could scour your databases for the most likely suspects. We're not telling you how to do your jobs, but for god's sakes, the job needs to get done."

"Time is of the essence, my friends," the leader of the INTERPOL IRT[4] insisted. "We must scramble Air Force units and initiate satellite scans of rural areas throughout France to locate the Mirage aircraft the terrorists were reported to have used. We have to notify the media and inform the public that these men are most likely ex-military who work in teams. They will have been extremely secretive and acting suspiciously over the past couple of months, working nights and not leaving any emergency contact information for anyone. Granted, we will be flooded with bogus leads, but we have no choice but to filter them out and take action where necessary in order to track these people down."

"Good old detective work," Bieber exhaled. "Works every time."

"I should hope my team is not the only ones in the thick of it," O'Shaughnessy replied.

"We will be setting up a command post here in the Palais," the DCRI deputy announced. "We encourage all of you to share whatever information you have with our crisis unit, and we will make all of our databases and resources available to everyone. Let us proceed with urgency and spare no efforts in ending this threat and apprehending these terrorists."

Shanahan and Gawain parked on the streets of Paris throughout the night, changing spots on the hour so as not to draw the attention of the police. Shanahan was able to refrain from being impaired by hydrocodone, taking a pill only when the pain grew intolerable. He used the pain to keep him sharp, pressing his wounds lightly when he felt himself nodding off. Gawain was taking amphetamines to keep awake,

---

3. Commandement des Operations Specialesor
4. Incident Response Team

and his respect for Shanahan grew as he appreciated the iron will it took for him to carry on in his condition.

"Y'know, boyo, once this is over ye might want t'look into volunteering for the Boy Scouts in yer spare time. I personally think ye'd make a helluva role model. Back in the day—,"

"Why don't you put a cork in it, you bastard?"

"Well, I'll tell ye," Gawain began, then sat up in alarm. "Holy shite, will ye look at that!"

"Not another tart you're fancying, damn you."

"No, the Tower! It's just as I said, will you look at it!"

Shanahan pulled himself painfully to an upright seated position and stared in astonishment at the scene ten blocks ahead of them on the Champ de Mars. They could see the Mirage hovering over the Tower with an oil drum suspended by a cable along its side. Police helicopters approached in the distance as the drum appeared to swing so that it got caught in the third level. They watched as four figures descended from a rope ladder and detached the drum from the cable. The Mirage suddenly began to rise despite loudspeaker warnings from the helicopters, and it ascended steadily before its jet engines sent it streaking off into the horizon.

"Here comes the cavalry, that's their arse now," Gawain chortled as a sortie of four jets streaked overhead in pursuit. "Turn on the telly, William, let's see what they're up to."

"The jets aren't going to shoot the bastards down over a populated area, it'd be a disaster," Shanahan switched on the TV on the dashboard. "They'll take evasive action until the terrorists make contact with the authorities. They'll coerce them to let the Mirage escape."

"All right," Gawain gunned the engine. "We'll get up close, you call Six and make sure they let me up. You be ready to get us out of here after I'm done. We've got another stop to make unless they blow us to hell."

"Why won't you tell me what the next stop is?" Shanahan demanded.

"And let ye steal my thunder? I'm going t'save the world again."

The BBC announced that four masked men in black uniforms were lowered from a VTOL aircraft along with an oil drum onto the third level observatory's upper platform at the Eiffel Tower. The police and RAID[5] teams were cordoning off a ten-block perimeter around the Tower and waiting for command vehicles to arrive. Police cars forced the BMW to a halt, and Shanahan managed to contact Six as Gawain was pulled from the vehicle and handcuffed. He harangued the police with insults as they helped Shanahan out of the car, inspecting his documents and contacting their headquarters for further advice.

"We just got word from the Palais confirming your identity," the police lieutenant returned Shanahan's wallet as Gawain was shoved against the police car and his handcuffs removed. "I suggest that someone take your partner aside and reeducate him on protocol."

"It wouldn't do any good," Shanahan winced painfully. "You need to get him up in the Tower. He's acting as a crisis negotiator. He may be able to persuade them to give themselves up."

"The man is a thug. Are you not going with him?"

"I got shot up at Bayonne last night, I can't make it. You've got to get him up there."

Nine hundred and six feet above the ground, the four Citadel mercs were busy at work implementing the next phase of their operation. Two of the men were prepping the thermobaric bomb for manual detonation as it sat wedged amidst a thick padding of americium. It was estimated that the explosion would have the effect of a dirty bomb in contaminating both the Tower and an area within a mile radius. The other two men remained on alert, watching the police vehicles converging below and the helicopters approaching from afar. Finally the team leader made contact with the police and began negotiating the transfer of the billion dollars to the Citadel account.

At once the mercs were startled by the activation of the Tower elevator. They had warned the police that any attempt to storm the Tower would result in them setting off the device via remote control at the

5. Recherche Assistance Intervention Dissuasion

touch of a button. Only when the doors slid open, they stared incredulously as the man known as Jack Gain stepped off.

"Well, ye've done a smashing job here, fellas," Jack said admiringly.

"How did you get up here?" the leader demanded.

"I was invited. I have a message from Chatillon, he got an order from the Queen."

"Chatillon! You have seen him?"

"Aye, we got caught by MI6 but managed t'escape. They brought us with 'em last night when they ambushed th' Russians. That bastard William Bruce was workin' with 'em, but he got his when the Mirage opened up on 'em. Chatillon's on his way back t'Carcassonne. He had me come up an' tell ye to set the bomb off."

"Set it off?" the leader asked incredulously.

"They need t'know we mean business. Th' Mirage'll be cleared t'pick us up in fifteen minutes. Ye set it up to go in twenty minutes, an' we'll have enough time t'get away."

"Destroy the Eiffel Tower," the leader said hoarsely. "We were told that would be a last resort. I will need some kind of confirmation."

"All right," Gawain nodded. "Let's try this."

With that, he drew his Glock from his waistband and shot the man in the face, the back of his skull opening like a tomato can onto the platform.

"All right, then," he waved the gun between the three remaining mercs. "Who else knows how to activate the bomb. You?"

"What are you doing, you sick bastard?" the merc raged at him.

"No, I guess not," Gawain replied. He fired his pistol again, and the man's brains spewed in an arc over the guardrail of the platform deck as he collapsed.

"So it's one of you two."

"It's a cell phone code, you fucking rat!" one of the mercs snarled at him. "Any of us could set it off. We weren't going to destroy the Tower unless they would've paid, and the Queen was sure that they would have."

"Y'know, that's the worst thing in th' world ye can call someone in this business, a feckin' rat. It really hurts, 'know."

Gawain always took time to file crosses into the tips of his bullets, which resulted in the shells fragmenting upon hitting a hard surface. As a result, a coin-sized entry wound resulted in a grapefruit-sized exit wound in many cases. It tore men's skulls apart, and within minutes the flow of blood made the platform area appear as an abattoir. Gawain tracked blood all the way to the elevator, and made his way back to the grade floor. When he got out, he was surrounded by automatic weapons and ushered over to where Shanahan sat in a courtesy wheelchair.

"You'll never learn, will you?" Shanahan shook his head. "The Yanks had their Chernobyl satellite focused on the Tower. They saw you execute all four of the terrorists. Now it's going to take a while."

"We don't have a while, Gummo. We've got to hit the road."

"What've you got in mind?"

"I'm pretty sure I know where the girls are. I'm also certain that it's where the nuke is. Call Six an' tell 'im we need backup, have 'em give us a transponder t'go."

"We probably won't need it. I'll just have Six tell the Yanks to put the satellite trace on us."

"Aw reet. Let's get a move on, we've got a seven-hour drive ahead."

"Seven hours driving? That's a lot of sitting time for me. Why don't we fly down?"

"We want t'give th' Russians time t' get a fix on us. They're permanent members of th' UN Security Council, they'll be able t'request information from the Yanks. Ye make sure they find out that we're heading t'Carcassonne. I'll bet ye all th'whiskey in Ireland they'll be on us as soon as we arrive."

"And what'll be the wisdom behind that, pray tell?"

"We're goin' to th' Citadel t'visit the Queen."

* * *

They reached the A61 shortly before dark, and continued along the Rocade Ouest onto the Route de Limoux. As they drove parallel along the Aude River, Gawain recognized the Pont Marengo bridge and crossed the Canal du Midi towards the railway station. He remembered Chatillon's men veering west towards the wooded area along the outskirts, and spotted the secluded road that led to the waterfall.

"We're being followed," Shanahan informed him.

"Aye, they picked us up on the Henri Gout," Gawain spied the waterfall ahead to his left. "They'll be here in about five minutes, an' they'll get directions in ten. Y'keep yer mouth shut an' let me do th' talkin' or we're both dead men. Stay in th' feckin car, got it?"

Shanahan was fascinated as Gawain turned off the road, bouncing down the incline and cruising straight into the small waterfall. He hit the windshield wipers and saw six men with Uzis standing in a semicircle in front of the vehicle.

"Don't shoot, it's Jack Gain," he rolled down the window and showed his hands before opening the door. "I was with Chatillon and his men at Montauban when we got ambushed by th' Corsicans. He called in and reported that th' European Council set us up. They were tryin' t' cut us out and deal directly with th' Russians. We cut a deal with William Bruce and made sure the Council smugglers got wasted along with th' Russians. Only we got hit by friendly fire. Chatillon was killed an' Bruce was wounded. He's in the car with me."

"This is far too much double-dealing and backstabbing, my friend," the leader stared evilly at Shanahan. "I believe we need to make this bastard tell us everything he knows."

"He got shot up in Bayonne backing me an' Chatillon. He's dead on. Th' problem we got is that I was followed here from th' Henri Gout. I think it's th' Russians. Chatillon suspected that th' Russians were gettin' info from the Americans' Chernobyl satellite an' figured out our hideout was hereabouts."

"Did you know our team at the Eiffel Tower was killed by the police?" the leader came around, taking a hard look at Shanahan.

"Aye. We just arrived from Paris. We saw the whole thing. We were surprised that ye moved that quick with the WMD, but we figured th' Russians were gonna press hard t'get their bombs back."

"This isn't making a lot of sense. How did you know to drive from Bayonne to Paris?"

"It wasn't rocket science, boyo."

At once an alarm sounded, a steady beeping accompanied by flashing red lights in opposite corners along the cave tunnels.

"It's the exterior alarm!" a gunman called out. "There's a breach along the perimeter!"

"I told ye," Gawain insisted. "The Russians are comin'. They're lookin' t'get their nuke back."

"Man your stations!" he ordered his gunmen. "Do you have a weapon, Gain?"

"Aye," Gawain drew his Glock and held it out. "I'll move this fella inside out of harm's way, then I'll reinforce yer gate guards."

"Very well. Let's get moving!"

"Aw reet, boyo, has that novocaine kicked in yet?" Gawain gave Shanahan a hand as he pulled himself out of the BMW. "If those Russians break through before MI6 gets here, it's game over."

"For God and country," Shanahan managed a smile. "That's your motto, isn't it?"

"Works for me every time, boyo," Gawain winked.

They could hear gunfire outside the cavern as the mercenaries began taking up positions at fortifications outside the waterfall. Two fire teams of eight Spetznaz troops emerged from a van outside the turnoff where Gawain had entered. They were armed to the teeth and were using grenades to rout the defenders outside the cavern. The explosions reverberated throughout the cavern and caused dust to trickle from the ceilings. Inside the throne room, the agents could hear the sound of muffled screams and squeals.

"It's the girls!" Shanahan's eyes widened. "They're here!"

Gawain raced into the throne room and saw the silhouetted figures of two women tied to straight-backed chairs against the far wall. He waved to Shanahan to follow him as he sprinted across the dais and shoved through a door behind the vacant throne.

He stood in astonishment at the sight of Lucretia Carcosa and Concetta Pinzone against the far wall of what appeared to be a well-furnished dressing room. It was undoubtedly the place where the Black Queen prepared for her receptions with his her Citadel soldiers. Jack was about to greet them just as Lucretia drew a pistol and shot Concetta in the left temple, causing her brains to spurt out onto the wall beside her.

"Thank god!" Lucretia exclaimed. "Reinforcements have arrived!"

"Nay, that's the Russians out there," Gawain said, watching Lucretia carefully as she held her Glock at her side. "They're chuckin' grenades at th' Citadel men out front. I don't think we'll be able t'hold 'em off."

"This woman is Concetta Pinzone, an assassin for the Sicilian Mob," Lucretia nodded at the corpse sprawled on the rug alongside her. "I worked alongside her while we were ambushed three different times by the Citadel. They finally made a deal with us to betray the Sicilians. We were instructed to bring those two women back here after rescuing them from the Corsicans."

"Ye've got a rear exit back there, don't ye?" he asked. "There's another corridor running back there. The bomb's back there, isn't it?"

"Yes," she said, watching Gawain's gun hand down at his side.

"Come on," he beckoned her. "The Russians followed me in here. We put in a call to MI6 but I don't know if they'll get here in time."

Gawain and Lucretia emerged from the back room, surprising Shanahan and the girls as he finished untying them. Both their faces twisted in anger at the sight of Lucretia.

"That's the bitch who kidnapped us!" they accused her.

"Why, that's our INTERPOL contact," Shanahan told them. "She's a double agent."

"William, meet the Black Queen," Gawain smiled softly.

"You bastard," she hissed. "You traitor!"

"Wait," Shanahan touched his fingers to his temples. "What in hell is going on here?"

At once a Russian charged into the throne room as his comrades laid down cover fire, retreating into the cavern behind him. MI6 had arrived minutes behind the Russians, who were suddenly caught in a bracket between the defending Citadel mercs and the MI6 team behind them. The Citadel mercs threw down their weapons before the MI6 agents, while the Russians ran inside the cavern to seek a means of escape.

The Russian leveled his weapon and fired at the figures by the wall alongside the dais. Shanahan tackled Fianna and Darcy, sending the three of them sprawling to the floor. Lucretia charged at Gawain, bowling him over as bullets raked her midsection. Gawain rolled and fired, cutting down the Russian as his comrades were pinned down by automatic fire in the outer alcove.

"Ye saved me," Gawain crawled up to her. "Why'd ye do it?"

"It's our code," she managed, her blue eyes growing cloudy. "All for one and one for all. You could never understand."

"Oh, yes I could," he saw the blood dampening the front of her black jumpsuit. "I've got a code I live by too."

"We need a medic," Shanahan said as he limped over, the girls crowding behind him as they stared in horror at Lucretia's wounds. "She's hit bad."

"Aye, I'm takin' her out th' back," he said, gingerly lifting her in his arms off the floor. "I'll take care of this th' best I can. The bomb's back there. Tell 'em we went chasin' after one o' th' Russians. Buy us some time, tell 'em they need to deactivate th' bomb."

"Did they prime th' bomb?" Shanahan stared at him.

"I wouldn't be here chattin' about it if they did," Gawain chortled, then blew a kiss at Fianna and Darcy. "You two take care of each other. I'll be in touch."

"What a bastard," Darcy hissed in disgust as they watched him disappear through the door with Lucretia in his arms. The three of them spun around as the Russians tossed their weapons to the ground and dropped to their knees, putting their hands behind their heads. The

MI6 rushed into the throne room, warily approaching Shanahan and the girls.

"I'd be careful going back there if I was you," Shanahan advised them. "I heard tell there's a nuclear bomb back there."

Chapter Ten

The MI6 agents took possession of the nuclear device and arranged for it to be picked up by the French Army. Shanahan and the girls were flown back to Paris before it was arranged for Fianna and Darcy to be taken back to America. Shanahan was admitted to a hospital where Morgana soon joined him. A hotel room was reserved for her shortly afterward, and the next morning Mark O'Shaughnessy and Joe Bieber arrived before she did.

"Looks like they'll awarding you another medal for this," Mark said as he sat at William's bedside. They had performed minor surgery to repair tissue damage caused by the 7.62 rounds that hit him on the dock at Bayonne. They kept him overnight as a precaution, and William would be leaving with Morgana when she arrived.

"Can't say it ever gets old," William smiled. "You should know, you've gotten far more than I ever will."

"I was decorated on the field," Mark reminded him. "Not quite the same as getting it from the Queen at Buckingham Palace."

"Let's hope this is the last of them under these circumstances," Joe interjected. "Two medals for preventing two nuclear attacks. If this went public, it'd probably set some sort of Guinness World Record."

"Perhaps this'll light a fire under the UN so they'll start clamping down on these nuclear nations," William grimaced. "First Iran, now Ukraine. Next time we may not be so lucky."

"So you think Gawain should be reporting shortly," Mark surmised.

"I have no doubt. He went deep undercover on this one. He got in with the Citadel, then he had people think he turned me against the European Council. It saved our cover, but I doubt I'll be able to use it again."

"Maybe he'll be able to help fill in some of the blanks. Those Citadel bastards are a tight-lipped bunch. The only reason they're not going to Guantanamo is because they're all former French military," Joe said ruefully. "They're all backing each other's story that they knew nothing about the Eiffel Tower plot or the nuke in the cavern. They're saying they got hired for guard duty by a corporate client. Undoubtedly they've got money behind them. If they get a high-powered lawyer, it'll be a challenge building a case against them."

"What about the Mirage?"

"They torched it on a beach along the coast," Mark shook his head. "They're real professionals. I don't think we've heard the last of them."

"What did you find out about Carcosa?"

"Not a whole lot," Joe shrugged. "They wanted to give her a desk job after she got shot in Poland but she threatened to resign. They called her bluff and she got some administrative leave before they called her back in. INTERPOL decided to give her some sort of special advisor status, which worked well for everyone considering her forte was interstate trafficking. Everyone you talk to seems unwilling to claim control over her, or lack of, as the case may be. She's a real lone wolf, or a she-wolf, if you will."

"She really ticked off those girlfriend of yours," Mark smirked. "They swore up and down that it was Lucretia who had them kidnapped. Nothing that a fistful of comps couldn't handle."

'There's the future missus," Joe said, rising as he saw Morgana walking up the hall. "Enjoy your stay. We'll see you soon."

"Congratulations on your upcoming wedding," Mark greeted her as they took their leave. "Take care of that rascal for us."

"I'll be expecting both of you to be there," she replied.

"Hello, darling," William kissed her lips as he rose from bed to retrieve his clothing. "I won't be long, we'll go have brunch somewhere."

"Are you sure you're up to it?" she was emphatic. "They said you got shot again. We can go back to the hotel and relax if you like. I wouldn't mind spending a couple of days pampering you. I took all my things out of the hotel at Toulouse, and Fianna's already gone home."

"It's not as bad as it sounds. I'm quite sure I caught ricochets. If I'd taken direct hits from 7.62 rounds, I'd be missing an arm and a leg. Jack did a great job stitching me up. They said he might have saved my life. Same as you did last year."

"Oh, don't remind me of that," she shivered. "Now, you said they gave you a desk position. Why on earth did you get sent somewhere to get shot at?"

"It's a long story, dear, I really don't want to go into it," he ducked behind a screen to put on his pants. "Let's just say they were short on experienced hands for what was required."

"Well, you need to start passing the buck, now that you're gonna be a married man. You've served your country, you got decorated by the Queen. Soon you'll have a family to think of. It's time to settle back and start thinking of the future. Gosh, sometimes you wonder how much of a future we have left. Did you hear about those terrorists who put a dirty bomb up in the Eiffel Tower yesterday? My goodness, that could've turned into a horrible disaster."

"Yes, it could've gotten really nasty," he agreed as he knotted his tie.

He placed an order with a nearby haberdasher to have clothes delivered to him, replacing the tattered gym suit he wore over the last two nights. He studied himself in the mirror and looked very much like the ladies' pet and the men's regret, the Gold Standard of MI6 who had set out on this mission a couple of weeks ago. He was going to have the most beautiful woman in Paris on his arm, and they would catch a cab to the Champs Elysees and have brunch at one of the finest restaurants. He was taking a reality check and coming out fine. The world of terrorist bombers, arms smugglers, mass murderers and serial killers like Jack Gawain, and psychotic mercenaries like the Black Queen and the Citadel would be far and away from him and his bride-to-be.

Along the ride to Champs Elysees he considered the political aspects of the path Great Britain had chosen. He ruminated over the fact that he had been called upon twice to risk his life in the greater interests of the United States of America. Had it finally come to this? Was the UK becoming a vassal state of the USA? Perhaps it was not quite that dire, but it seemed whenever the US barked these days, the UK bit. The UK followed them into every one of their wars, and was now following them into the shadows of their War on Terror. The American President said that that era was over, yet here he was on the field fighting their demons once again. Even worse, he was fighting them alongside a serial killer like Jack Gawain. Would he ever be called to account for all the people he had murdered? Would it take a massacre of innocent civilians before he was ever taken to task?

"You're so quiet, baby," Morgana leaned her lovely head against hers, and he could smell the scent of her perfume as he rested his cheek against her hair. He wished he could stay her forever, just come to an eternal peace with this blessed angel in his arms.

"Just thinking, love," he kissed her head. "It's been a long week."

The cab pulled up in front of the Dominique Bouchet restaurant on the rue Treilhard, and Morgana was pleased by the bare wall ambiance complemented by expensive works of contemporary art. They found a cozy table in a corner where they opted for the tasting menu along with a bottle of blush wine. The waiter started them off with beef gely, a pig foot, foie gras and coco bean cream. Morgana took a bite of French bread with the foie gras and thought it quite heavenly. William decided to get the pig foot off the table.

It was said that Napoleon Bonaparte was of Corsican descent, and to native Frenchmen the Corsican dialect sounded somewhat Italian. It had gone the way of the Gaelic language in the UK, and was hardly ever spoken except by older people in Corsica. William did not speak French very well but was growing used to the Corsican language after having stung them twice since last year. He knew it was highly unlikely that the word had not spread from the Citadel to the Corsican Mob, even though the Citadel was probably was at war with the Corsicans by now. Gang wars were far too expensive to prolong, and it was possible that even the Corsicans and the Sicilians had made the peace by now.

That meant that the man known as William Bruce might well have a price on his head, and the Corsican accent he heard at a table a couple of rows across from theirs made him break a cold sweat. He tried to focus on the conversation but the three women at the table behind Morgana were so boisterous that he could barely hear the other patrons next to them. It was impossible to tell if it was the patrons or the waiter were speaking in the dialect, or both. As the waiter passed by he glanced at William, and there was no way to tell if it was look of recognition or intent.

"Mmm, this was such a good idea," Morgana said as they were next served the roasted sea bass with artichoke and orange butter. "Now I know why people are always talking about French cuisine. Their sauces certainly make a difference. I know that they have special schools for sauciers, you know, the chefs who specialize in sauces."

"Yes, the lobster sauce comes next. I'm certain it will be quite wonderful."

He wondered how they would set up a hit in broad daylight in a place like this. Most certainly they would crush the Corsican Mob for pulling a stunt like that on the Champs Elysees. It wouldn't do William a damned bit of good, and probably traumatize poor Morgana to the end of her days. Would the waiter call it in, report to a higher-up that the accursed William Bruce was dining at Dominique Bouchet? Would they send in a ringer, dress a gunman in a waiter's uniform and have him walk up to the table to do the work? Or would it be done at curbside from a passing car? Maybe they would even wait for him to go to the restroom.

"William, you're so quiet. I know you must be tired. It was selfish of me to ask you to go to brunch after having surgery just last night. Why don't we just leave?"

"No, no, my darling," he insisted. "A man would be absolutely mad to pass up the opportunity to take you to brunch. Just seeing you across the table from me makes it all go away. You're the picture of loveliness, I could gaze into your eyes forever."

"Oh, come on," she blushed, lowering her eyes.

Just as she did, the waiter fumbled with the silverware as he set the table alongside them. William's fingers darted towards his Glock in his ankle holster and was a nanosecond away from popping it loose. The waiter muttered an oath in Corsican, then caught himself as he looked over at William. He gave a sheepish grin, then quickly set the table and walked off.

"Perhaps we can go back and relax afterwards," he agreed. "I'm sure I'll be far more chipper for dinner this evening."

"Maybe we can lie down and see what pops up," she said saucily.

"You're quite a tease," he chuckled, greatly relieved that nothing had happened to give his fiancée the shock of her life.

Morgana Mc Laren became a May bride, officially becoming Morgana Shanahan on May 7th. They got married in London, so that her estranged relatives did not attend. And so it was with William, who would not marry in Belfast as he did not wish to decide between the Catholic Church of his relatives or the Protestant Church to which he converted in the social climb of his youth. Some of his colleagues, including Mark O'Shaughnessy, attended as did Morgana's friends from the airline. Fianna was her maid of honor, and William chose a friend whose life he had saved in Afghanistan. William knew that, unless by chance, outside of holiday cards they would probably never meet again.

Their first domestic issue came about when they had to decide on a place to live. They spent their first week in his apartment, but he wanted them to have a house, a place she could claim as her own. He began surfing the Web for areas around England but was increasingly perturbed by the rising wave of social unrest in the streets of London. The Islamic mosques appeared to be growing more militant, causing a backlash from white activist groups such as the National Front. He did not want to expose Morgana or their future children to that, so they decided to leave England for somewhere less volatile.

The next choice was the East Coast in the USA. New York City was far too expensive, and Fianna was already looking for a new roommate after they gave notice in letting go of their Central Park apartment. Only the better areas along the entire coast had been devastated by floods, hurricanes and global warming so that the Jersey Coast was as a wasteland and Virginia's coastline not much better. They would next consider somewhere in Europe for a place to live.

Only Italy seemed like a dangerous place due to William's skirmishes with the Mafia over the last year. The political scene in Germany seemed as rambunctious with the pushback of right-wing neo-Nazi groups arising in protest of the wave of Islamic immigrants arriving from the Middle East and Africa. Too many people might have been curious about William in Austria, and Morgana thought Eastern Europe might be too risky and too cold. France was starting to look like the best place by default.

Their sex life was just awesome, and it was as if his entire objective was to please her in every way he could. She began noticing that he would wait until she climaxed five times before releasing himself, and considered how her married friends complained about their own husbands performing their duty as if relieving one another. She was fairly certain that they would never descend to such a dismal relationship.

What did bother her was how he seemed to slip into a melancholy at different times during the day. Sometimes he would stare out the window as if he was in another world. Other times she would see him reading the newspaper or a book, and lapse into a reflective state during which he stared past the written word into the wall or the floor. She would tease him and he would grow playful, yet she realized he was merely flipping the switch in the dark room where his mind had retreated to.

They rented a room in Paris, and agreed that they would remain there for the time being until they found a home in the suburbs. She grew fond of window-shopping around the city and decided it would be a nice place to live. They went out to eat for breakfast, lunch and dinner, and she realized they would have to find a house soon so that William's money did not continue leaking down the drain.

One day he asked where she would like to go for the evening. When she said she had nothing particular in mind, he suggested Carcassonne. The name made her tummy clench as she knew it was where Fianna and Darcy had been rescued from kidnappers. Only William went on about how beautiful it was at night, and she did not want to disappoint him. She dressed to the max in a midnight blue dress suit, and they drove their rented Mercedes early that noon so as to reach the region of Languedoc-Roussillon by dark.

They rented a room for the evening, then made reservations at L'Escargot Restaurant. She noticed how they insisted they had no tables before he went into his black book. After a couple more calls, everything was fine. She realized the black book was the secret place in his life that she could never be part of. He spoke to people in muted tones about shadowy places and things she would never see. She knew he would never betray her; her major concern was that the dark world would swallow him up one day.

Upon arriving at the restaurant, they were allowed access and escorted to a cozy table in a far corner. They ordered the oysters in hollandaise sauce and the duck breast skewers along with a bottle of wine. William was in a fine mood after the seven-hour drive and joked about the snooty patrons and their airs of entitlement. She was always impressed by how much his attitude had changed. She had always suspected him of being class-conscious, even a bit of a social climber, but he seemed to have gotten past that as if it was not how he wanted her to perceive him.

She saw a couple dressed in black, the man wearing a bowler derby, granny sunglasses and a suit. The woman wore a dress suit as if dressed for a funeral. They looked over at Morgana and William, exchanged comments, and came directly over to the table.

"How now, William and Morgana. What a pleasant surprise."

"Jack. I thought you fell off the face of the earth. Morgana, this is Lucretia Carcosa. She's with INTERPOL, she'd worked with us on our last assignment."

"My pleasure. Congratulations on your wedding, I heard all about it."

"Why not have them pull up a table for us? We wouldn't mind some fine company."

"Well, I'm not sure they'd accommodate us in a place like this."

"Oh, I'm quite sure they will," Jack grinned. "After all, nothin's too good fer yer blushin' bride, or the Black Queen."

Lucretia narrowed her eyes momentarily before breaking into a tinkling laugh. The three of them shared a knowing look, and suddenly it all flooded her: the bulletins on the news of weeks ago, the terror threat, William having been shot... the Black Queen.

All of a sudden she felt as if transported through time and space, into some strange and dark dimension. She found herself sitting at a table with people who looked like those she thought she knew, but didn't really know at all.

Dear reader,

We hope you enjoyed reading *The Citadel.* Please take a moment to leave a review, even if it's a short one. Your opinion is important to us.

Discover more books by John Reinhard Dizon at https://www.nextchapter.pub/authors/john-reinhard-dizon

Want to know when one of our books is free or discounted? Join the newsletter at http://eepurl.com/bqqB3H

Best regards,
John Reinhard Dizon and the Next Chapter Team

The story continues in:

Cult of Death

To read the first chapter for free, please head to:
https://www.nextchapter.pub/books/cult-of-death

About the Author

I began my so-called career at the age of six, writing dialogue for my stick-figure cartoons. I actually began reading at the age of three, a God-given talent that my parents attested to. Upon entering first grade I refined the technique of expressing words in print, and from there it progressed. By sixth grade I wrote my first novella, a James Bond ripoff called *Enemy Ace.* It was about a WWII German pilot, Fritz Hammer, recruited by the CIA to thwart a negriphile named Blackman. Umm... yeah. Well, guess what? Fritz Hammer appeared in *Tiara* a half century later, and the plot morphed into *The Standard* shortly thereafter. Hmm.

I continued writing through high school, spending one summer writing a 1,000-page epic about the USA turning fascist and starting WWIII. I pulled it in a tad and wrote a second spy novel featuring Fritz Hammer. I lent both of them to two of my teachers and never got them back. At this stage of my life, I am certain that none of us will ever profit from those long-lost treasures.

It really kicked in during my twenties while I was masterminding my punk band, the Spoiler. I wrote a ten-novel series on Richard Mc Cain, a Special Forces superhero in Vietnam. They were action-packed, well-researched classics that never saw the light of day in the pre-Internet days. Mc Cain became the hero of *Bloody Sunday*, an apocalyptic Northern Ireland saga. Again, an awesome piece of work that never went anywhere. Mc Cain became the protagonist of my Christian novel *Abaddon (Destroyer)*, so it wasn't all in vain. I also wrote a half-dozen sci-fi space novels, great action tales that never got published.

When I relocated to Texas, I went through another writing phase which sowed some major fields. I wrote *Hezbollah*, which got published a quarter-century later, as did *The Bat* and *Both Sides Now*. There was also *Tiara*, which was an offshoot of a sci-fi novel I wrote back in NYC. I was really gearing up to make something happen, but that didn't progress until I moved to Missouri.

I ended up going to bed with Publish America, a vanity press rip-off that ended up with some of my best work. They got *Tiara*, then *Wolfsangel*, followed by *Cyclops* and *Penny Flame*. It took four years before I realized they weren't paying me a dime and never would. I decided I had to make a last-ditch effort to make something of my so-called career, and 2013 was the year.

I devoted myself full-time to getting published and put thirty novels on the market. Some were self-published, and many others went to indie lit publishers. I've had over two hundred reviews of my work posted on Amazon. Over eighty percent are five-star reviews. I haven't made any decent money yet, but my readers have made it worthwhile.

What keeps me going? The great, incomparable stories, the awesome characters, and the satisfaction of knowing you are writing things that people will appreciate long after you're gone. I can pick up one of my novels after years of not having read it, and become absorbed by it all over again. I wonder why they never reached the heights that so many farce novels find in Hollywood. I'm not gonna worry about it. My readers know and I know. 'Nuff said.

All I can say is: pick up a JRD novel and see what you think. If you really think it sucks, just write me an e-mail and tell me why. Odds are I'll send you your money back. Or if you're in Kansas City, I'll buy you a beer.

Oh, yeah, and I give all the credit and glory to my Lord Jesus Christ. He put the spirit and the vision inside me. If He didn't like what I was doing, He would've taken it away a half century ago.

And I'm glad He hasn't.

Also by the Author

- The Nightcrawler Series
    - Nightcrawler
    - Tryzub
    - The Plague
- Generations
- King of the Hoboes
- Strange Tales
- Penny Flame
- The Standard
- The Test
- Tiara
- Vampir
- Wolfsangel

The Citadel
ISBN: 978-4-86750-721-6

Published by
Next Chapter
1-60-20 Minami-Otsuka
170-0005 Toshima-Ku, Tokyo
+818035793528
14th June 2021